DELLA

J.J. STARLING

To contact the author, you may email her at:
info@sallyjling.com

Cover designed by Andy Massari.

ISBN: 978-1-7371329-9-8

TABLE OF CONTENTS

DELLA

CHAPTER 1

Palm Beach, Florida
1932

She sashayed into my office on a hot steamy Monday morning before I'd even had my first cup of joe, her hips swaying to some Caribbean beat only she could hear. Conservatively over the top would be how I'd describe the rest of her—a black velvet hat perched on obsidian hair, a net veil drawn to her chin, and a high-necked, black dress hugging a killer figure from her ample bosoms to her slender ankles. A stole dangled over one shoulder as though it were a dishrag—who wears mink in the middle of summer in Palm Beach?—and her gloved hand held a foot-long, rhinestone-encrusted, black cigarette holder. A thin ribbon of smoke curled into the air; ashes sagged at the tip of the lit tobacco.

Her sashay ended at my desk.

"Is this the Marlow investigating firm?" Her high-pitched, nasally voice befitted her appearance.

Netting from her hat veiled hazel eyes accented by long false eyelashes and dark blue eyeshadow, cheeks painted bright pink, and full lips thickly plastered with lipstick—ruby red. Her perfume—I couldn't tell if it was the expensive variety or some cheap flowery stuff from a nickel and dime—permeated the air like a heavy mist.

I stubbed my Chesterfield into the overflowing ashtray on my desk, jumped up, and firmly nodded.

"Yes, ma'am. Drake T. Marlow, at your service." My father, an attorney for thirty-five years, always greeted people with his ancestral British/Irish-style demeanor—at least the first time. He said the introduction set the tone for the entire encounter.

"Good. May I?" She gestured her cigarette toward a wing-back chair in front of my desk.

"Of course," I said. "Please, sit down."

She lowered her delicate frame into the chair and crossed her legs. My eyes bulged as the slit in her dress parted, revealing perfectly shaped legs. They reminded me of the ones I saw in France after the war. The ones belonging to Danielle. The ones I couldn't forget.

Finding my ashtray, she tapped the end of her cigarette holder. Ashes dutifully dropped into the receptacle. Her presence held my gaze as I sat.

"What can I do for you, Miss—"

"Carmichael. *Mrs.* Stanley Carmichael." She drew on her cigarette and blew a plume of blue haze into the room. "At least I was until two weeks ago; now I don't know who I am."

Obviously, the woman knew who she was, she just told me—Mrs. Stanley Carmichael. Was this some kind of joke?

I sat forward and leaned my arms on the desk. In a voice laced with skepticism and concern, I said, "Mrs. Carmichael, you don't know who you are?"

"Yes. I mean, no. My driver's license says I'm Mrs. Carmichael, but I'm not sure that's me." Her lower full lip formed a pout.

"I'm confused. If you're not Mrs. Stanley Carmichael, then who are you?" I asked, spreading my hands.

Her eyes narrowed behind the veil, sending me a scathing look. She uncrossed her gams, stood, and said, "Aren't you the private investigator? Isn't it your job to ask questions and find out these things?" With her cigarette holder dangling from her mouth, she pulled open her black leather clutch and extracted a roll of greenbacks. Peeling off a half dozen C-notes with great flair, she tossed them onto my desk. "Do your job," she commanded. She turned and walked out of my office with the same sashay she walked in with, her cigarette still sporting ashes.

Stunned, I stood and tucked both thumbs under my green suspenders. Caressing them, I wantonly eyed the dough occupying center stage on my desk—more than I'd seen in months! The office rent was due, and my bank account was down to a few bucks, not to mention Betty Lou hadn't been paid in a month and was about to abandon me. The money certainly would come in handy, but this dame was wacky—she knew her name but not who she was. Did I really want to get involved?

As I turned to gaze out the window, my right eyebrow spiked at the scene. At the curb, Mrs. Stanley Carmichael folded herself into a blue Lancia Astura, an expensive Italian ride. Suddenly, she didn't seem as wacky as I thought.

Turning back to the Franklins, I didn't think twice. I gathered the bills and stuffed them into my pocket.

CHAPTER 2

"Hey, did you see that broad? She looked like male bait if there ever was any. And those high heels! Making a red hot statement." Betty Lou clucked her tongue as she strolled to her desk.

"What does that mean?" I walked to the opening between our offices, leaned against the door jamb, arms crossed, and eagerly awaited my secretary's explanation. With Mrs. Carmichael's other attributes holding my gaze, I hadn't noticed the color of her shoes.

"It means, Mr. Naive, that *broad* was furious at the guy who died." Plump, middle-aged, and dressed professionally—blue skirt, white collared blouse—Betty Lou gave me a 'you should know that' smirk. She moved to the filing cabinet and stuffed the third drawer with her bagged lunch and purse.

"Just how do you figure that?" I'd never been accused of knowing a woman's mind. Not that of Danielle nor the one I was to marry in Atlanta. She ran down the church aisle into another man's arms just as our vows were about to be exchanged. That was five years ago. Since then, I've remained a confirmed bachelor.

"By her outfit, she's obviously a widow. But not a typical one. A typical widow would have worn black shoes out of respect for her deceased husband. This broad wore red. A sure sign of passionate anger." Betty Lou turned to her desk and sat.

"Hmm. I'd never have figured that. But the color of Mrs. Carmichael's shoes shouldn't make any difference. It's the color of her money that's important." I walked over and dropped two one-hundred-dollar bills onto Betty Lou's desk.

Her blue eyes—her best physical feature by far—widened, and her jaw dropped. "You mean she's our client?" Betty Lou picked up the bills and turned them over. "They're not counterfeit, are they?" She held each up to the light as though, by doing so, she could tell.

"Yep, and nope. The woman claims to be Mrs. Stanley Carmichael. Then again, she's not sure. She wants me to find out."

"Huh?" Betty Lou scrunched her face and circled an index finger at her temple.

"Yeah, crazy, but that's the gist of our meeting—short, to the point, and unorthodox. But money talks. And right now, Mrs. Carmichael's money will get me out of the doghouse with you and let us stay here for a few more months."

"Good thing. I was afraid I'd have to help you pack up the office." Betty Lou tucked the bills into an envelope and slid the packet into her top desk drawer.

"Pay the landlord and take what I owe you from what's left. There should be plenty for both, with some left over. I'll keep the rest for expenses during the investigation."

Betty Lou placed fists on her broad hips. "What you really mean is you'll use what's left to bribe your informants into doing your work."

"Hey," I said, taking offense. "The client doesn't care how I get the truth? Just that I get it." I walked toward the door in a huff.

"Okay, Boss, this is your show. But I don't mind telling you I wouldn't touch that broad with a ten-foot pole. Mark my words, she's a fireball waiting to explode, and her red shoes? They're the color of blood; they give me the willies." Betty Lou's shoulders shook as though she shivered.

Her cautionary statement was overly distrustful. Wasn't it?

I plucked my white straw hat from the coat rack, kissed two fingers of my right hand, and brushed the fossilized megalodon shark tooth next to the door for luck. Then I walked out.

CHAPTER 3

"Morning, Mr. Marlow. Here are your morning papers." Willie, a slightly built colored man in his sixties wearing a white short-sleeve shirt, an apron over khaki pants, and a tweed Boston Scally cap, stood on the sidewalk outside his newspaper stand at the corner of Worth Avenue and Hibiscus, a short block from the office. *The Palm Beach Post* and *Miami Herald* dangled from his scarred outstretched hand.

"Thanks." Though the two papers only cost four cents, I exchanged a dime for them.

Willie gazed at the coin. "My, my. Why such a generous tip today? You come into a windfall?" He dropped the dime in his apron pocket before I could change my mind.

"Something like that. Say, Willie, you ever hear of a Stanley Carmichael?"

If anyone knew the goings on in the Palm Beaches and who was doing what, Willie did. He'd had his stand on Worth Avenue ever since Addison Mizner and Paris Singer built the prestigious and private Everglades Club that opened in January 1919, catered to the Palm Beach elite, and dominated the Worth Avenue skyline. Since then, he'd sold newspapers to the rich and famous and listened to every word traded between residents and visitors who frequented the club and high-end Worth Avenue stores like Tiffany and Gucci.

He knew where the illegal booze came ashore, heard so much female chatter that he could write his own gossip column, and eavesdropped on the secrets of where to put money in the stock market. He'd invested wisely and taken his money out before the stock market crash of '29. Now, he and his family were living comfortably off the proceeds. Far more than most people, including myself.

"Stanley Carmichael," Willie repeated. He scratched his head, causing his cap to tilt at an angle. "Ain't he the guy who bought the farm a week or so ago? By the size of his obituary, he didn't have much influence in Palm Beach circles. It was only two short paragraphs."

"I guess I missed it."

Even if the obit were there, I'd probably have skimmed right over its two paragraphs since I'd never heard of Stanley Carmichael before today. He wasn't even on the periphery of my envisioned circle of Palm Beach influencers like Post cereal heiress Marjorie Post, the Mar a Lago estate owner, or Robert Redinning and his influential friends from Philadelphia.

"I've probably still got the paper somewhere if I didn't already use it to wrap the garbage. I can look through my stash if you like."

"That would be wonderful. But I'll take a raincheck if the print harbors eggshells and rotting banana peels."

Willie let out a high-pitched chuckle. "No sir, no banana peels for you."

"Seriously, please let me know if you hear anything about Carmichael." I took out a dollar bill and handed it to

Willie. He knew there'd be more where that came from if he supplied me with quality info.

"Was that his widow I saw coming out of your office earlier?"

"Yeah. She's now my client."

Willie let out a wolf whistle. "Quite the bombshell!"

Betty Lou had called her a fireball. Willie called her a bombshell. Both words indicated potential detonation. Had those two collaborated on their vocabulary?

"I guess. Don't forget to let me know if you hear anything."

"You got it, Boss." Willie gave me a two-finger salute.

CHAPTER 4

I returned to the office and hung my jacket and hat on the coat rack. Betty Lou abruptly stopped typing and peeped at me over her reading glasses. She was a saintly woman who had worked for my father before he retired, and my parents took off for an extended European "vacation of a lifetime." I came home from my job as a detective with the Atlanta PD to see them off, but Betty Lou wouldn't hear of my returning to the big city. She said after my stint as an M.P. during the war, all the crime in Atlanta, and my regrettable experience at the altar, I belonged back home among family and friends. She then talked me into opening this office with her as my assistant.

I knew starting a business during the Depression was a gamble, but then that's why I chose Palm Beach to locate my office. Those that lived in the fashionable town always had dilemmas and money. That combination made my decision much easier. We'd been in business for only a few months—a few very lean months.

"By the looks of the sweat circles on your shirt, you've been talking to Willie. How many times have I told you to move into the shade when you talk to him? In this scorching Florida heat, you could get sunstroke." Betty Lou shook her head, clucked her tongue, and huffed out a sigh. "Some people never learn."

"I wore my hat, and I don't need a mother; I have one," I barked. "What I need is an intelligent and clever assistant who knows when to mind her own business!" I swiftly walked toward my office, head high, nose up.

"Then I guess I should have minded my own business instead of uncovering valuable information about your mysterious Mrs. Stanley Carmichael while you were kibitzing with Willie."

I jerked to a stop mid-stride. Retracing my steps, I stood before Betty Lou's desk and dug into my pocket. I set a peace offering on top—a half-melted lemon cough drop.

"Won't work," she said, turning back to her typewriter.

"Until?" I asked sardonically.

"Until you apologize for hurting my feelings." Betty Lou continued to pound away at the keys.

"Just what are you typing?"

We hadn't had a client in weeks, even though Marlow Investigations stood in an ideal location, discretely tucked into a two-room nook at the side of Foremost Fashions, an exclusive shoe store in the heart of Worth Avenue, where I bought my white summer oxfords.

Betty Lou removed her reading glasses and looked up. "I'm typing notes on my findings."

She zipped the typing paper from her machine and offered it to me. When I reached out, she snatched the paper away.

"Nuh-huh. Not until you apologize." She narrowed her gaze and set her mouth in a pressed thin line.

I rolled my eyes.

"A-pol-o-gize," she slowly repeated, emphasizing each syllable as though I hadn't heard her.

I took a deep breath, held it, and then let it out slowly. "Okay. I'm sorry. You can mother me any time you want."

Truth be told, Betty Lou was like a second mother to me and my younger sister. We'd known her since childhood when she started working for our father's solo law practice. For all practical purposes, Betty Lou was a member of the family. After her husband died, she spent holidays with us, celebrated birthdays, attended my graduation ceremony from the police academy, and my almost wedding.

Once again, I held out my hand.

Betty Lou handed me her typed notes. As I digested the words, my eyes grew wide.

Ugh!

I hated when Betty Lou one-upped me with a large side serving of crow. But I should be used to the foul-tasting bird by now. Her network of business owners and domestic help working for some of the most elite inhabitants from one end of the high-class island to West Palm Beach on the mainland was remarkable. All she had to do was pick up the phone. Between her and Willie, they could earn a substantial living through blackmail. The thing was, they both had scruples. Me? I'd bent the rules a time or two, but never enough to cross the line into arrest territory. At least not yet.

"So, Mrs. Stanley Carmichael, with the first name of Della, is a professional Palm Beach playgirl whose husband loaned her out for special occasions? With him dead, who's paying for her upkeep?" I eyeballed Betty Lou.

"You're the one with P.I. behind your name. Do your job and start asking questions. But I don't think 'Della' hired you to find out who's footing her bills. She hired you to figure out who she is."

"Discovering who's laying out the cash for her livelihood may uncover the person behind her person," I said, in an 'I know how to do my job' tone.

"Sounds like a tongue twister. But, seriously, Boss, since you're bent on taking this case, against my warning, I might add, you must concentrate on finding her real persona. That's what she paid you for. What I gave you there is a start on your journey." Betty Lou pointed the earpieces of her glasses at the notes.

I gazed at the paper and flicked it with my fingers. "This would be far easier if we could access Della's birth certificate."

"I agree, Boss, except we don't know her maiden name or where she was born. Without that, the only way to find the information is to hike up to Jacksonville and look through every birth record from the year she was born. Trouble is, we don't know that either."

"Right. I'll be off then." I grabbed my jacket and fedora, laid a finger kiss on the shark's tooth, and exited.

My first stop would be the Green Turtle, a bar and grill on the ocean a few blocks from the office. Betty Lou's note said Mrs. Carmichael used to frequent the establishment. In the six months I'd been back, I hadn't recalled seeing her there, and she was impossible to miss.

CHAPTER 5

With its gigantic polished turtle shell mounted outside the entrance, the Green Turtle sat on the west side of Ocean Boulevard, the road that paralleled the Atlantic Ocean down the east coast of Florida. Tom Wellington, a local guy, and Kalef "Cookie" Koa, the Australian chef, owned the restaurant. I'd become buddies with Cookie in France when we met at a bar after the war. He was my age, and we'd shared several exciting European adventures together before I shipped back to the U.S. I'd even talked him into coming to Palm Beach, believing he'd do well here. That I know of, I was the only one who knew his actual background. Had that information, become public, Cookie would not have been able to open the restaurant, let alone live on the exclusive island.

Because of his blond hair, blue eyes, refined features, and light skin tone, no one knew he was a multigeneration aboriginal from Australia. He said his skin tone was due to Euroasians mixing with his aboriginal ancestors back in the 1700s when England used the southern Pacific island as a penal colony, thus the difference in his skin color and features. None of this bothered me, but the information would have become scandalous among the island's residents had they gotten wind of it.

At ten o'clock in the morning, I walked through the back screen door and entered the kitchen. No one was in the Green Turtle except for Cookie and the prep cooks.

"G'day, mate," said Cookie in his typical Aussie accent. "Ready for some turtle fritters? I'm trying a new recipe. A little spicier than normal." He used a wire skimmer to scoop up several golden tidbits from hot oil and show them to me.

I looked at my watch. "Too early in the day for me, my friend, but I'll come back tonight now that I know you have turtle on the menu. Can't miss that."

The Green Turtle restaurant was known for scrambled turtle eggs, turtle soup, and turtle steak in season. With the establishment across from the beach where giant green, loggerhead and leatherback sea turtles came ashore to lay eggs, Cookie easily obtained turtle eggs and meat. But the delicacy was only available during turtle laying season—May through October—when the turtles came ashore. Cookie believed in turtle conservation and harvested only a limited number after the female laid her eggs, so it was hit or miss when Cookie served up the sea creature. While tourists didn't come to Palm Beach much during the summer, locals from as far away as Miami packed the joint between March and October, despite the Depression once word got out that Cookie had turtle on the menu. Or was it because of the secret liquor room hidden behind the bar?

"Well, if your visit isn't for fritters, it must be for drum." Cookie occasionally used Australian slang, leaving me the chore of interpretation.

"Drum?"

"You know, mate, 'information.'" Cookie continued to drop pieces of the battered turtle into the simmering oil.

Knowing the Green Turtle was a hot spot for local gossip, I leaned against a prep table, ensuring I didn't get in the way of the cooks slicing lettuce and tomatoes, and said, "I'm in desperate need of some drum."

"Okay, mate, what's on your mind?"

"A Mrs. Stanley Carmichael, Della Carmichael. You heard of her?" I asked.

Cookie and the prep cooks instantly stopped what they were doing and, like statues, stared wide-eyed at me. They reminded me of Lot's wife when God turned her into a lifeless pillar of salt for disobeying him and looking back at Sodom.

"What?" I asked, gazing between the men.

Cookie let out a whistle. "You sure can pick 'em."

"What does that mean?"

"It means, mate, she's one hot potato you might want to let cool indefinitely." He returned to his fritter-making. The prep cooks side-eyed each other and then continued their chopping.

"Can't do that. I've already accepted Mrs. Carmichael as a client."

Cookie put down his wire spoon and wiped his hands on a towel. "Let's jaw at the bar, and I'll tell you what I know."

I followed Cookie through the kitchen to the front of the restaurant, a wooden structure that looked out over the ocean. We each sat on a stool at the bar, now rarely used for its original intent because of Prohibition. Thankfully, the fan was blowing directly on us cause I knew this would be a sizzling conversation.

Cookie rubbed his hands together as though hesitant to speak. When he raised his eyes, they had a glazed, faraway look. I'd seen those eyes before.

"You know her, don't you? And I don't just mean her reputation. I mean, you *know* her. Intimately." I met Cookie's gaze.

"Look, mate, that was before she became Mrs. Stanley Carmichael and long before you returned from Atlanta."

I was stunned but tried not to show it. "Just how many years ago was that?"

"Over two years. She used to frequent the Green Turtle with Paris Singer."

"*The* Paris Singer? Former President of the Everglades Club and heir to the Singer sewing machine fortune? I thought he was married to Lillie."

"Was and still is, as far as I know. But bein' married didn't stop him from havin' an affair and child with the famous dancer Isador Duncan over two decades ago. I guess Paris was still lookin' for love when he met Della. After a judge dismissed charges against him for real estate fraud a few years back, he and Lillie returned to Europe. Della stayed."

Even though I was in Atlanta then, I remembered reading about the scandal. When the bottom fell out of the Florida real estate market in the mid-1920s and the Everglades Club went into receivership, Singer was arrested for real estate fraud when he couldn't pay loans, for which he used the failed club as collateral.

"And that's when you two got together?"

"Lasted only a short while until Della met Carmichael. That was the end of us." Cookie dropped his gaze.

I wanted to ask him if what was under the black dress was real, but I didn't have the heart. Besides, I respected his apparent remorse that the relationship went south.

"What happened, Cookie? You're a handsome, charming guy."

Cookie looked up. "Tom and I were just startin' the restaurant. Carmichael had—" He rubbed his thumb and fingers together to indicate 'money.'"

"What was her name then before she became Mrs. Stanley Carmichel?" I asked.

"Della Smith."

Smith? She couldn't have had a more common last name if she'd tried.

"Hmm. Mrs. Carmichael seems confused about who she is and has asked me to find out. Anything else you can tell me?"

"Not about her name, but I heard a rumor she had somethin' to do with her husband's death."

My brows shot up. "A black widow?"

"Hey, Cookie, shipment's here. They need your John Hancock," yelled one of the prep cooks from the kitchen door.

"Be right there," Cookie called back. "Gotta go, mate. I hope you find what you're lookin' for. Come back for dinner." He gave me a pat on the back.

As I returned to the office, the sun beat down even hotter than before. Perhaps that was because I now had a black widow as a client. Maybe that's what her outfit meant—black for the widow part, red shoes for the blood on her hands.

CHAPTER 6

As I approached the office, I pulled Betty Lou's notes from my jacket pocket. The next person I wanted to speak with was Constance Grimly. She lived across the Intracoastal in West Palm Beach and had been Della's roommate. How Betty Lou discovered this tidbit was a mystery, but her research skills were as good as any P.I. Dad used to refer to her as a "bulldog" and "the best researcher he knew." That's why I agreed to this suggested arrangement—that and the fact that she'd work without pay during the lean months.

Sliding into Celia, my 1927 Chevrolet Series AA, I engaged the engine. Top down, despite the blazing sun—I'm a glutton for punishment, but I like the wind in my hair—I drove to West Palm Beach. Most people get confused by the parallel cities, thinking they're identical. But anyone visiting the area knew there was a vast difference.

Developing the island of Palm Beach started when Standard Oil tycoon Henry Flagler extended the Florida

East Coast Railway south from Jacksonville to the Palm Beaches. Arriving on the mainland in 1894, that same year, the Flagler-built hotel Royal Poinciana opened on the island of Palm Beach, turning its swamps and jungles into a winter resort for the wealthy. The Breakers hotel followed in 1896, as did Flagler's residential estate, Whitehall. To house the hotel workers, Flagler further developed the city of West Palm Beach.

Miss Grimly's place of work was Woolworths on Clematis Street. Located in the heart of West Palm Beach, the dime store sold everything from aspirin to stuffed toy zebras and included a popular diner. I parked on a side street, strolled in, and grabbed a red leather seat at the soda fountain counter. An elderly woman—gray curly hair, a pencil stuck behind her ear, and "Irma" on her nametag—approached.

"Young man, what can I get you?" She wiped the counter in front of me with a damp cloth.

"Root beer float. And the whereabouts of Miss Constance Grimly. I understand she works here." My parched throat looked forward to the cool, tasty refreshment as I gave Irma my best smile.

"Constance, huh?" Irma pulled the pencil from behind her ear, wrote down my order on a pad, then gazed at me with wary gray eyes. "You a relative? Boyfriend?"

"None of the above. A friend of a friend."

"Well, she's on break just now. I'll tell her you're here. Whom shall I say is calling?" Irma sounded like the gatekeeper in one of the Palm Beach estates.

"The name's Marlow. Drake T. Marlow." I extracted a business card from my wallet and handed it to her.

Worry lines creased Irma's brow. "A private investigator? Is Constance in some kind of trouble?"

"No, nothing like that. I want to ask a few questions about a friend of hers."

"I'll be right back," said Irma, holding up my card. She walked the length of the counter and slipped into the kitchen behind a swinging door.

I tapped impatient fingers on the counter, drooled over the apple pie, coconut cake, and oatmeal cookies under glass cake domes, and sighed. The question I asked myself this morning about Della Carmichael still rolled annoyingly through my noodle—did I want to get involved?

A woman with bright blue eyes, blonde hair, and a figure just shy of Della's walked out the door carrying a tray with a root beer float. For the first time since being jilted, my heart fluttered.

"I'm Miss Grimly. I understand you wanted to speak with me." Her voice was soft like an angel's, and her movements graceful as she positioned a delicate hand around the root beer glass and placed the float in front of me. Her face was makeup free and flawless. I guessed her age at twenty-two.

"Uh, yes," I said in a mesmerizing fog as I gazed at her plump lips. "I—I'm Drake T. Marlow. I wanted to ask you some questions about a friend of yours."

"And who might that be?"

Her piercing eyes, the color of the shallow aqua ocean, seemed to hypnotize me into silence.

"Well?" Her brows peaked, waiting for my answer.

"Oh—sorry, yes, the name of the friend. I believe she calls herself Mrs. Stanley Carmichael."

"You mean Della?" Constance's eyes grew as wide as her broad smile.

"Yes, Della. I believe you were roommates before she married Stanley."

"Yes, but I haven't seen her in ages. She's okay, isn't she?" Her forehead crinkled.

"As far as I know. I just saw her this morning."

"Whew. You scared me there for a minute. After Della married Stanley, she moved to Palm Beach. I guess she got too sophisticated to spend time with a lowly waitress at Woolworths. I never heard from her again. Too bad, 'cause I really liked her."

"How long did you know her?"

"About a year."

"I understand her maiden name was Smith, Della Smith. Is that correct?"

Constance pulled back. "Smith? I don't think so. Her last name when she roomed with me was Brown, Della Brown. You sure we're talking about the same person?"

Carmichael, Smith, and now Brown. No wonder Della didn't know who she was.

"Yes, I believe so—black hair, married Stanley Carmichael a couple of years ago?"

"Sounds like the same person, but I knew her as Della Brown, not Smith." Constance gave me a skeptical gaze.

"Hmm. Well, what can you tell me about Della Brown?"

"Let me see." Constance brought an index finger to her cheek. "She was full of life, I can tell you that. And she loved to dance. I never saw a woman move her hips like Della. It was so—sensuous—like watching her make love to the music. Know what I mean?"

"I do," I said, thinking about how her hips swayed when she entered my office this morning.

"Do you know where she worked?"

"Sure, at Ocean Ballroom. She worked weekends. That's where she met Stanley."

"Did you ever meet Stanley?" I asked.

"No. Della was very private about their relationship."

"So you don't know his occupation, where he came from, things like that?"

"Uh, Mr. Marlow, you might want to drink your float. The ice cream melted." Constance jutted her chin at my glass. The ice cream had become a cloud of white floating on the soda, creating a frothy crust.

"Sure," I said, placing my lips around the straw and sucking up the savory taste of root beer mixed with vanilla ice cream.

"I need to get back to work," said Constance.

The counter and tables were beginning to fill with the lunch crowd.

"I may need to ask more questions. How can I get in touch with you?" I asked.

"I'm here, Monday through Friday, 7:00 a.m. to 3:00 p.m.," said Constance, gesturing at the counter.

I paid for my float, left a generous tip, and grabbed my hat.

~~~

"So, Mr. Investigator, learn something important?" Betty Lou was finishing her lunch—ham and cheese on rye, carrot sticks, and coffee—remnants still visible on her desk when I walked in.

"You know I did. And you probably know what it was, Miss. Smarty Pants. You could have told me and saved me a trip."

"But then you wouldn't have met Constance." Betty Lou gave me a shrewd grin.

"Granted, she alone was worth the trip, but it still feels like I fell off my horse only yesterday. I'm not sure I'm ready to get back in the saddle just yet."
~~~

"Look, Boss," said Betty Lou, hands on hips. "You're handsome, intelligent, single, and dress well." She nodded at my tan suit and crisp white shirt. "Constance is beautiful, young, and single. There's no reason you can't take it slow and see where the attraction goes."

"I'll think about it, but I don't even know if she's attracted to me."

"That may well be, but the man has to take the first step. Now, what are you going to do about our client?"

"I have one more stop. Then I think it's time to pay Mrs. Stanley Carmichael a visit."

CHAPTER 7

Ocean Ballroom sat at the east end of Banyan Boulevard. The road, known for its plethora of speakeasies and brothels, had seen some high times before and during Prohibition. In fact, one of America's most famous women—Carry Nation—even walked its streets decades earlier.

I was only nine when I heard my mother say, "The lady with the reputation for chopping up speakeasies with a hatchet is coming to town."

Dressed in black, Nation made her way up and down Banyon Boulevard carrying a Bible and touting scripture in hopes of shaming men into turning from their wicked ways and stopping their patronizing of saloons. She also wanted them to vote to turn local municipalities from wet to dry. That she had escaped an alcoholic husband and abusive marriage only added to her determination. In retrospect, I gave the lady and her "Hachetation" campaign credit for her strength of character and persistence. Still, more than a decade later, the passing of the Nineteenth Amendment hadn't gone over well with the American people.

With the Depression now upon us, many former establishments on Banyan Boulevard had gone belly up. The exception was Ocean Ballroom, a lively dancehall that still serviced a brisk crowd looking for companionship, good music, and a place to dance. I arrived late afternoon. Bing Crosby's popular tune "At Your Command" spilled out the opened doors.

"I'd like to speak with the owner," I told the hatcheck girl.

"Mr. Wilson's in his office. Up the stairs, second door on the right." She pointed to the stairs across from her.

"Thank you," I said, tipping my hat.

Before climbing the stairs, I peeked through the window in the door to the dance hall. Several entwined couples waltzed about the room. Half a dozen lovely attired and made-up ladies sat in chairs on the far side, waiting for clients to come in. Men bought tickets—ten cents a dance—selected a partner, and hit the floor.

"Mr. Wilson's that way, mister." The hatcheck girl scowled and jabbed her finger toward the stairs while chewing a wad of gum.

"Right," I said.

Leaving the window, I climbed the steep stairs to the landing and found the office. Straightening myself, I removed my hat and knocked.

"It's open," cried a gruff voice from someone who sounded preoccupied.

Upon opening the door, a man in a white shirt blotched in sweat with sleeves rolled up to his elbows hovered over a desk covered in stacks of papers. Two fans blew hot air around the room, fluttering the sheaves held down by paperweights—a book, coffee cup, and scissors.

"Mr. Wilson, I'm Drake T. Marlow, a private investigator. Have a few minutes? I'd like to ask you some questions."

Mr. Wilson, a weaselly-faced man with sharp features and dark beady eyes, looked up and eyeballed me over his spectacles. "What kind of questions?"

"About a former employee of yours. Della Carmichael. I believe her name was Della Brown when she worked for you."

Wilson removed his glasses. "I know a Della, but not one with the last name you mentioned." He sat back.

"This Della married Stanley Carmichael. Does his name ring any bells?"

"Carmichael, huh? Yeah, I remember a Stanley Carmichael. A regular customer around here until about two years ago. He stopped coming when he married one of my girls, but her last name was Warren. Della Warren."

"Black hair, hazel eyes, killer figure, loved to dance?"

"Sounds like her. But then, all my girls love to dance. That's why I hire them." He gave me a smug smile.

"This one had something special. Once the music started, her hips swayed as though she invented the beat."

"Yeah, that was Della Warren, all right. A sassy little broad and some kind of dancer. Something happen to her? Is she in trouble?" Wilson sat forward and licked his lips as though waiting for some salacious tidbit of gossip.

"She's a client. I'm trying to understand all I can about her background."

"If she's your client, why don't you just ask her?" Wilson raised his thin brows.

"Yes, that would be the conventional way to do things, but this is a complicated case. Anything else you can tell me about Della?"

"Naw. She came, attracted a lot of business for me, then met Carmichael and left."

"Do you know where she was from or where she worked before?"

"If memory serves me correctly, she danced in a hall somewhere in central Florida. Tampa or Orlando, maybe."

"I've heard rumors she may have been involved with her husband's death. Know anything about that?"

Wilson let out a sinister laugh. "Which husband?"

I blinked hard, wondering if I'd heard him correctly. "She's been married before?"

"Did I fail to mention she was a widow when she danced here?"

"I guess you did." Not much surprised me in my line of work, but everything about Della Carmichael, or whoever she was, surprised me.

"Well, I gotta get back to work; sorry I couldn't be of more help. Please let yourself out." Wilson put on his glasses and focused back on his paperwork.

"Right."

When I returned to my office, I wasn't sure whether I was defeated or invigorated by this new information.

"Well? Find out more about Mrs. Stanley Carmichael?" asked Betty Lou as soon as I entered the office.

"Don't you mean Mrs. Della Warren?" I slipped my jacket and hat onto the coat rack.

"What? She's been married before? How many names can one woman have?"

"I don't know, but I intend to find out."

I pulled the phone book from the bottom drawer in my office and dropped it onto my desk. Thumbing through the pages, I found Mr. and Mrs. Stanley Carmichael. A phone number accompanied her address at 323 Seabreeze

Avenue, a short drive north of the office. I thought about phoning ahead, but catching people off guard usually worked best when I wanted to ask a few questions. That way, their gestures were more spontaneous, and they didn't have time to make up and rehearse their answers.

I'd have gone over there tonight, but I was beat from today's running around, and besides, I promised Cookie I'd get back to the Green Turtle for dinner. First thing tomorrow morning, though, I intended to get some answers from the only person who had them—Mrs. Della Carmichael, also known as Della Smith, Della Brown, and Mrs. Della Warren.

CHAPTER 8

The following day, I started my chariot, and off I went from my one-bedroom guest house discretely tucked behind Keith and Helen Jorgenson's bungalow. Snowbirds from Philadelphia, the couple allowed me to stay in the cottage in exchange for caretaker duties.

When I first returned to Palm Beach, I stayed in my parent's house in West Palm Beach, which was fine for a while, but I wanted to set up my office in Palm Beach since that's where the wealthy clients were. And I wanted to live close by. The Jorgensons, former clients of my father's, offered me a deal I couldn't refuse—stay in the cottage rent-free in exchange for overseeing their home while they were back in Philadelphia.

So far, everything had run smoothly, though one never knew when the lawn maintenance crew wouldn't show, a water pipe would spring a leak, or the swimming pool would turn green with algae. That's why I was there to ensure that whatever issue occurred would be handled quickly. We had a symbiotic relationship that worked well for the Jorgensons and me.

Fifteen minutes later, I parked outside a stately two-story stucco home in the middle of a residential neighborhood dotted with Mediterranean-style homes. I figured Addison Mizner designed and constructed this one since he built dozens of homes in Palm Beach before his company went belly up.

I used the door knocker at the arched entranceway to announce my presence. A few seconds later, a petite Asian woman opened the door. Her appearance took me back a half dozen or so years to the story of James Horace Alderman, also known as the Gulf Stream Pirate. He'd smuggled Chinese citizens into Florida's west coast long before he turned to rumrunning on the east coast.

If this woman had been among those smuggled into the country, she was one lucky lady to have made it to Palm Beach. Tales of Alderman charging exorbitant prices to smuggle Chinese foreigners into Florida only to divert delivery to the Florida Straits, where he dropped off his passengers in shark-infested waters, had circulated for years. Alderman's career ended in 1927 when the Coast Guard caught him on his schooner while running rum into Florida. During a scuffle with the Guard, Alderman fatally shot Robert Webster, a government agent. Tried and convicted, Alderman died in a botched hanging at Coast Guard Base 6 in Fort Lauderdale after being convicted of first-degree murder.

"Yes?" said the woman, peering at me with dark, wary eyes.

"I'm Drake T. Marlow to see Mrs. Della Carmichael." I handed her my business card.

"She expecting you?" The woman spoke in broken English.

"I didn't make an appointment, but she'll see me. Please tell her I'm here."

"You wait," said the woman, gesturing with her hands. She closed the door.

I gazed around the well-manicured property—precisely clipped hedges, bordered flower beds, and the grass cut to an even height. Was Mrs. Stanley Carmichael this precise in all her dealings?

Suddenly, the door opened.

"She see you. Please come." The diminutive woman bowed slightly, then stepped back to allow me to enter. "This way." She took small shuffling steps as she led me through the finely adorned foyer of decorative glass and porcelain vases, down a long hall embellished with oil paintings of portraits and landscapes, and into a back room decked out like a salon.

A manicure station took up space on one side of the room with polishes and nail files nicely arranged. A rolling cart covered with towels and various colored creams beside a reclining chair filled the other area. In the middle was a massage table where Mrs. Stanley Carmichael lay face down. A white towel wrapped around her head like a turban, covering her hair, while another draped over her bare derriere. My eyes scanned the rest of her raw curvaceous form, sending me into a lustful fog.

"Mr. Marlow, I hope you have some good news for me." Mrs. Carmichael's high-pitched voice pierced the mist.

"Umm—yes, ma'am. You asked me to find out who you are."

"That's right. And?" asked Mrs. Carmichael without getting up or turning to face me.

"And I have. So far, I've found out you're Mrs. Stanley Carmichael, Della Smith, Della Brown, and Mrs. Della Warren. Care to tell me which one you really are?"

Mrs. Carmichael let out a haughty laugh. “That’s all you have for me? A bunch of names? I hired you to find out who I am.”

I let out a sigh. “Look, ma’am, I’ve been all over Palm Beach County, tracking down your old acquaintances. Each gave me a different name. I’d appreciate a straight answer. I’m a bit weary of playing games.”

“Games? Is that what you think? That I hired you to play games?” Mrs. Carmichael suddenly reached back and grabbed the towel. She pulled the covering discretely around her body in one rhythmic gesture as she turned over and sat up. One hand held the ends of the towel together at her considerable cleavage while her long, shapely legs dangled off the table. A pea-green beauty mask covered her face, exposing only her eyes and lips.

I gasped.

“What’s the matter, Mr. Detective? The assignment too difficult for you? All I did was ask you to find out who I am. What do I get in return? A bunch of names and whining! So you’ve had to do a little running around and digging. Isn’t that what you were paid to do?”

I was sure the lady’s cheeks flushed with anger, but I couldn’t tell with all that gunk on them. Her eyes narrowed to slits in her olive green face, reminding me of a green anole lizard common to these parts. I stifled a chuckle, then regained my composure.

“So, you’re not going to answer my question?”

We stared at each other, waiting for the other to cry, “Uncle.” Neither did. Frustrated, I turned for the door.

“Wait! Wait!”

I could tell by her trembling voice she was close to tears. I hated when a woman cried. I reluctantly turned back.

Mrs. Carmichael captured my eyes in her tear-filled ones. Suddenly, she didn't seem tough and demanding at all but a vulnerable little girl looking for answers.

Then unexpectedly, she opened her hand and released her grasp on the towel. The cloth glided dramatically from her ample bosom, down her silky abdomen, and mounded softly around her thighs like a snow drift.

I'm not a prude and enjoy gazing at a beautiful woman like any other man. But Della Carmichael was volatile, and the ten-foot pole Betty Lou suggested wasn't anywhere near long enough.

"So, this is how you entice men into doing your bidding and not answering their questions? Well, not this one!"

I turned and walked out the door without looking back.

CHAPTER 9

Shaken, I returned to the office with Della's image—green face perched atop the most seductive body I'd ever seen—seared into my conscience. Upon entering, I slammed the door. The glass rattled loudly, almost breaking.

"I don't want to be disturbed," I growled at Betty Lou.

She looked up in surprise as I stepped into my private office and slammed that door, too. Tossing my hat onto a chair—it immediately rolled onto the floor—and wriggling out of my jacket, I plopped into my desk chair, needing perspective on what just happened.

To get that, I pulled a glass and silver flask, a monogrammed gift from my father, from my bottom drawer. Two fingers of bootleg whiskey seemed the right amount. The liquid burned from my mouth to my stomach as I gulped it down. It was only ten o'clock in the morning. What was I doing?

I sat back, emotionally exhausted, and took a long breath. Holding it, I let it out slowly. Again. Again.

"Betty Lou," I chirped.

She opened the door and sheepishly looked around its edge. "Is it safe to enter?"

I motioned her in and gestured for her to sit in one of the chairs. She came in carrying her steno pad and pen. I returned the glass and flask to the drawer. Then I changed my mind and put them back on the desk.

"I think I'm gonna need your ten-foot pole—with extensions." I laced my fingers behind my head and leaned back.

"So, not the plum job you had in mind?"

"Not by a long shot. And I might have just blown it." I lit a cigarette.

"Want to tell me what happened?" Betty Lou set the tablet and pen on her lap.

I sucked on my cigarette and blew smoke into the room as I relayed my visit, still annoyed I hadn't accomplished my goal of getting Della to admit which last name was hers.

"Uh, Boss, I forgot to tell you. Mrs. Carmichael called just before you got back."

I sprang forward in my chair, my muscles tightening. "What?" I stubbed out my cigarette.

"Yeah, she said to tell you she's sorry for what happened and wants to meet you tomorrow at Woolworths. Said she'll explain everything then."

"Humph." I crossed my arms over my chest and turned up my nose.

"I guess she's trying to make amends for whatever set your teeth on edge. If nothing comes of your get-together, at least you'll be able to see Constance again."

"You're right," I said, slapping the desktop.

"That's the spirit!" said Betty Lou. "Always look on the bright side and turn lemons into lemonade." She picked up her tablet and pen and rose. "She said to be there at 2:00 p.m."

"Wait a minute. I thought you were against my taking this case. Now you're for it?" I couldn't figure that one out.

"You got it wrong, Boss. I'm not for Della. I'm for you seeing Constance, and if this is the only way to get you there, I'm for that. It's time you settled down. Betty Lou gave me a wink and returned to her desk.

I poured two more fingers' of whiskey into my glass.

That night, I tossed and turned, unable to make heads or tails out of Della Carmichael. She wanted me to find out who she was, but she was unwilling to tell me which one of the names I turned up was hers. Now she's ready to confess? Nothing fit. I needed to do more digging before meeting her tomorrow afternoon.

~~~

Early in the morning, deprived of a good night's sleep, I figured a few laps of the pool would wake me up and prepare me for the day. I preferred to swim in the buff since I was the only one at the house, and no one would see me behind the tall, neatly trimmed eight-foot fichus hedge that surrounded the patio. Entering the pool area, I tossed my towel onto a chaise lounge and dove in.

Ahhh.

With the sun not yet breaching the roof of the house, the cool, shadowed water refreshed me, and I swam a few laps to get my circulation going. Then I turned over, shut my eyes, and floated on my back. My mind drifted to Della, then Constance. Other than their similarity in build, they were opposite sides of a coin. Della was shapely, provocative, and undoubtedly alluring but poisonous as a
~~~

coral snake. She made my brow pucker and tongue feel like I'd sucked on a lemon. Constance, too, was curvy, but that's where the similarity ended. She had a soft voice, full lips, and a pleasant personality. The thought that I'd see her again in a mere seven hours brought a smile to my lips and sweetness to my tongue as though I were savoring cotton candy.

Lost in my musings, I was abruptly thrust back to reality when I found myself shoved underwater. When I opened my eyes, the water swirled above me as I sunk below its surface. Hitting the bottom of the pool, I pushed off at an angle. Breaking the water's surface, I gasped for air only to find a skimming net used to remove leaves from the pool plopped over my head and pressing down on my shoulders, preventing me from escaping.

What the—

While treading water and gulping for air, I noticed a brute of a man standing on the pool deck, a revolver tucked into his waistband. He held the end of the long wooden pole to which the skimming net was attached. Taking a breath, I submerged, swam a few body lengths, and then resurfaced. The net splashed around me again, holding me down and immersing me to my neck. While I tried to push the net off, being in the deep end of the pool and unable to touch the bottom, I had little leverage against the man with broad shoulders and all muscle.

"Stay away from Della," he ordered in a voice like rough sandpaper.

"I'm not the one who started this. She is," I retorted. I rapidly blinked as water dripped into my eyes from the net.

"Yeah, well, she made a mistake. Keep away from her, or you might find yourself permanently at the bottom of the pool next time." The man flipped the net off my head, tossed the wooden pole onto the deck—resulting in an ear-splitting *thwack*—and strode out the gate before I could even make sense of this.

Gathering my wits, I swam to the pool's shallow end and scrambled up the steps. Though adrenalin surged through me, I cautiously loped across the pool deck and out the gate, hoping to catch Blutos' license plate. When I got to the street, the car's brake lights were disappearing around the end of the block, and Rupert, the gardener from across the street, stood perched on a ladder, ready to trim hedges. As I waved at Rupert, he looked curiously at me and then let out a robust laugh. Suddenly, I understood why. I was standing in the middle of the street in my birthday suit, leaving nothing to the imagination. I quickly hand-covered my privates.

"Hey, Rupert, did you happen to see that car?" I tilted my head in the direction of the disappearing vehicle.

"No, sir. Came out just before you did."

I nodded, then turned back toward the house. Now I was mooning Rupert. My only consolation was he, not Sylvia, the housekeeper, was the one who saw me. Otherwise, I might have been heading to Chattahoochee, Florida's state mental hospital near Tallahassee, the state's capitol. I'd heard of people being sent there for far less.

On my way back to the cottage, I couldn't wait to meet Della at Woolworths. In no mood for games, I had plenty of questions for her, and after my encounter with Bluto, she owed me some answers.

CHAPTER 10

"Looking forward to your meetings this afternoon?" Betty Lou was emptying the trash when I arrived at the office.

"Which one?" I placed my hat and jacket on the coat rack, then waited for an answer.

"Both," she replied.

"Well, if it weren't for the fact that Bluto tried to drown me this morning and delivered a dire warning for me to stay away from Della, I'd say, 'yes.' But thinking back to the incident, 'no.' I'm not looking forward to my meetings."

Betty Lou gazed at me stone-faced, openmouthed. "You're joking, right?"

I shook my head. "No joke."

She dropped the trash can, wrapped her arms around me, and squeezed. "Are you alright?"

"I'm here, aren't I?"

"What in the world happened?" She gave me the once over to see if I had any injuries.

I recalled the blow-by-blow encounter.

"We need to call Chief Borman and report this." Betty Lou rounded her desk and picked up the phone.

"Wait! Let me meet Della first. If this guy, whoever he is, finds out someone's inquiring about him, that may get back to her, and she might not show. "

"Good thinking, Boss." Betty Lou put down the phone. "So, you didn't get a good look at the car?"

"Nope. But I'd recognize the moose if I saw him again."

"Describe him."

"Around six feet, round face, bulbous nose, thick lips, muscular build, dressed nicely in an expensive suit. Oh, and the guy had a scar on his left cheek."

"His left cheek! Just like Scarface Capone! But he's in Alcatraz, serving his sentence for income tax evasion. Besides, he doesn't do the dirty work. He has his thugs do it for him, so maybe it's one of them."

"Maybe," I said, shrugging.

"But what would they be doing fifty miles north of Miami Beach? And what's their link to Della Carmichael? Do you think it has to do with bootleg whiskey? No, it couldn't. I haven't heard of The Outfit servicing Palm Beach, but one never knows. Early tomorrow morning, I'll check with my network." Betty Lou hastily wrote herself a reminder.

"Fine. Just let me get through today and my rendezvous with Della."

"What about Constance? I hope you're still looking forward to seeing her."

Though my heart quickened at the mention of her name, I had mixed feelings, so I ignored the question altogether. "I've got some research to do. I'll be out the rest of the day."

"Well, check in with me later. I want to ensure Bluto hasn't made minced meat out of you before your meeting."

I rolled my eyes. "I'll be fine. I plan to take Marvin with me in case there's trouble."

"I wish you wouldn't," said Betty Lou, biting her lip.

"Between the two of us, we'll be fine."

"Yeah? When's the last time you went out with Marvin?" She crossed her arms, challenging me.

"Umm, just last week," I lied.

"Well, don't come whining to me if something happens."

Just then, the phone rang. Betty Lou shooed me off as she went to answer the call.

I walked into my office to make plans for the day—my first stop to be the county tax collector's office. I wanted to know what the taxes were on Della's house and who owned it. Harry Ringblatt, the Palm Beach County tax collector, was an old high school chum who was a whiz with real estate and numbers. I'd seen him several years ago when I visited my parents but hadn't seen him since. Catching up with him would be nice. I'm sure he'd provide all the information I needed, including a dollop or two of pertinent gossip.

Not knowing what the afternoon would bring, I transferred my full flask of whiskey from the desk to my inside jacket pocket. I never knew when I might need a nip or two. And with this case, that could be any time.

~~~

I arrived at the Palm Beach County Courthouse, a stately neo-classical building that housed all the county government offices, and parked out front on Dixie Highway. Climbing the building's broad steps, I entered through double glass doors and located the stairs to the second floor.
~~~

Down a long corridor, I entered room 206 and stopped at the counter.

"I'd like to see Mr. Harry Ringblatt. We're old friends." I handed my card to an elderly clerk.

He raised an eyebrow as he gazed at the card. "I'll let him know you're here."

Ambling through several desks, the clerk made his way back to a private office. Half a minute later, Harry strolled out.

"Drake, you ole' son of a gun. Where have you been keeping yourself? Come on back." He pointed to a swinging access half door. "Hard to believe I haven't seen you since you returned to town."

"Yeah, well, I've been trying to get my business up and running." We shook hands, and I followed Harry back to his office—a small space with glass halfway up the walls and blinds covering them. Harry sat behind his sizeable worn desk. I sat in an equally worn wooden chair facing him.

"So, how's it going?" Harry seemed all smiles.

"You've had another kid," I said, spying the photo of his wife and three children—two boys and a baby girl—on the credenza behind his desk.

"Didn't you get the announcement? Patty Ann. Isn't she precious?" Harry reached back, grabbed the photo, and handed it to me.

I gazed at the smiling baby. "She sure is." I returned the photo to Harry, hoping his childbearing prowess hadn't rubbed off on me.

"When are you going to get married and have a family? All our classmates have taken the plunge, so I can't understand how a good-looking, intelligent guy like you has stayed single all this time. Why hasn't some Atlanta or Palm Beach beauty hasn't gobbled you up?"

"Oh, I've had my opportunities," I said, remembering the near miss. "But I guess I'm just not the marrying kind." I wasn't about to share my sad story about being ditched at the altar.

"Maybe with the right woman, you'd think differently." Harry gazed back at the photo, misty-eyed.

"Perhaps," I said.

"So, what brings you here? I know it's not just my charming personality."

One thing about Harry Ringblatt, he wasn't your typical stuffed shirt county employee. He had replaced his father when the elder Ringblatt suddenly became too ill to continue working. With intimate knowledge of the county and riding on his father's impeccable reputation, Harry was a shoo-in for the position. Sure, he knew and was serious about the real estate and appraisal business, but more than that, he was a genuinely nice guy.

"Actually, I'm working on a case. That's why I'm here."

"Oh?"

"Yep. It's confidential, so I can't tell you much about it, but I do need some information from your office."

"How can I help?"

I pulled a piece of paper from my pocket. "This is the address of a home in Palm Beach, along with the current resident's name. I need to know who owns the house, what the taxes are, and who pays them." I handed the paper to Harry.

He gazed at my scribbling, then pushed a lever on his intercom. "Mrs. Simmons, please come in."

In no time, Mrs. Simmons entered. She was a sharp-faced middle-aged woman with glasses perched atop her head. Harry gave her the piece of paper, asked her to research the property owners and taxes and return with the answers post haste.

"Carmichael. The name sounds familiar. Didn't he die a few weeks ago? I believe I read his obituary in the Post," said Harry.

"Same guy," I acknowledged. "Know anything about him?"

Harry sat back. "Can't say I do, except what the newspaper printed, but I overheard the girls gossiping last week that his wife may have had something to do with his death. If that's true and you're in any way involved with her, you probably need to watch your back."

I'd now heard that her first husband had died and that Della may be involved in Stanley's death from two unrelated sources. Were the two spousal deaths related? Was there any truth to her involvement? If Bluto was trying to keep me from finding out by threatening me to stay away from Della, Harry was right—I did need to watch my back. Then again, that's why Marvin was going with me this afternoon. He was an excellent deterrent to trouble.

After a few more minutes of chit-chat, Mrs. Simmons entered Harry's office and handed him a piece of paper.

He thanked her, read what she'd typed, and gave me the report.

"Well, here it is. I hope it helps."

I took the paper and read the information. Owner – Stanley Carmichael. He also paid the taxes. If he and Della had been married for two years, why hadn't he put her name on the title?

"Exactly what I was looking for, Harry. You're the best."

"Does the information surprise you?"

"Seems like everything I've turned up regarding this investigation surprises me. Then again, it doesn't. This is one bizarre case."

"Perhaps you'll fill me in someday when it's over."

Harry and I shook hands before I left the office. My next stop was the Palm Beach Police Department. I wanted to know the real scoop about Stanley Carmichael's untimely death.

CHAPTER 11

Palm Beach Town Hall, the town's government building, housed the Palm Beach Police Department and two-room jail. Since it opened in 1925 while I was in Atlanta, I hadn't been in the new building or visited since my return. Now, however, I needed their services.

As I entered the building, a large vinyl-covered open room greeted me. A three-foot-high railing ran down the middle of the room, and on the working side of the barrier, officers staffed the semicircular reception desk and an adjacent dispatch area. Behind the desk stood a tall card catalog cabinet with dozens of drawers. I surmised the cabinet held index cards with pertinent information about case files. On the reception side of the barrier, two wooden benches, more like former church pews, offered seating. A photo of Chief Borman and the Palm Beach Police Department crest hung on one wall.

"How can I help you?" asked the officer behind the desk.

"I'd like to see Chief Borman. I'm an old friend." I handed the officer my business card.

When I was a teen, my father hunted bears with Borman west of Jupiter. According to Dad, Borman used a Winchester rifle, his only weapon, to bag his prey. The chief didn't even carry a handgun on the job, using his bigger-than-life persona to quell difficult situations.

"I'll let him know you're here." The officer picked up the phone, dialed a number, and spoke to Borman. A few minutes later, the chief entered.

"You look just like your old man. Come on back, and we can talk in the office. By the way, how are your folks enjoying Europe?" asked the bespectacled chief with alert blue eyes and a receding hairline.

I followed the Chief through the low swinging door in the railing and down a corridor. "Got a postcard from them last week—Paris. I'm sure they're strolling the Champs-Elysees hand-in-hand and watching the sunset from the Eiffel Tower."

"They deserve the trip. Your dad worked hard. I hope they have a wonderful time." Borman and I sat next to each other in front of his desk. "I see you're a P.I. now."

"Yep. Several years as an M.P. in the Army and a detective on the Atlanta police force was enough for me, but it was really Betty Lou who talked me into returning. She's my assistant now. A smaller town and making my own hours is appealing, but it's awfully quiet right now."

"Just wait til season. You'll be wishing for the dog days of summer again," said Borman with a laugh. "But you can't go wrong with Betty Lou or establishing a business in a town like Palm Beach. It's served me well all these years."

Known as "Mr. Palm Beach," Joseph Borman first served as Marshall when the town incorporated in 1911. When the police department formed in 1922, he became the first police chief. Ten years later, Borman still functioned in that capacity. He knew everyone, and everyone knew him.

Not hard to do in a town with a population of just over 1,700, especially when he'd been there as each resident moved in. But because of his longevity in the area, he also knew most folks in West Palm Beach, including the Sheriff, attorneys, and residents.

"So, what keeps the police chief busy these days on the island? No doubt rumrunners."

Borman let out a friendly laugh. "Yeah. It's been a dozen years since Prohibition started, and I'm still occasionally tracking down smugglers in the waterways. But it's unlike those early days. Then, it was small everyday guys running boatloads of whiskey into Florida. They kept me hopping and weren't easy to catch. Now, we've got the big guns like Capone's Outfit and the other hoodlums from the northeast running booze up the coast. The Feds do most of the work, though, now that the Coast Guard has the means to stop their boats."

"Times change. I understand in the early days before Prohibition, you were the chief cook and bottle washer in Palm Beach."

"You could say that. Back then, I was tax collector, fire chief, voter registrar, code enforcement officer, and secretary of the Town Caucus. It was a small community, and I wore lots of hats. I only wear one now, but it keeps me busier than ever, even with my thirty additional officers. But you didn't come to talk about the good 'ole days. How can I help you?" "I'm working on a case and wanted to get some information about the death of Stanley Carmichael. I believe he died a couple of weeks ago."

"Tragic situation," said Borman, shaking his head in empathy. "Mr. Carmichael was soused and decided to go for a swim. He passed out and drowned."

My eyes widened, and an alarm went off—a swim, almost downed? My encounter with Bluto in the pool this morning seemed curiously similar. Were the incidents connected?

“Foul play?” I asked.

“None that we found, but there were small rectangular bruises on both his shoulders. We never could identify where those came from. Any suggestions?” Borman gazed at me curiously.

I shrugged. “I heard rumors that Della, his wife, might have been involved in his demise. Any truth to that?”

“I doubt it. Mrs. Carmichael was out with friends the afternoon he died and found him floating in the pool when she got home. Her friends confirmed her alibi.”

“And she never left their company for any extended time?”

Borman leaned toward me. “Are you suggesting she might have slipped out, gone home, killed her husband, and returned to be with her friends before anyone noticed her missing?”

“I’m not suggesting anything, really. Just asking questions.” I didn’t want to sound confrontational.

“Well, I don’t think that’s possible. We took statements from Mrs. Carmichael’s lady friends. None of them said anything about her leaving.” Borman sat back.

“Do you remember who the friends were? Or where the group was when Mr. Carmichael drowned?”

The chief scrubbed his chin. “Not off-hand, but I can check with records and call you later. By the way, why all the questions? What’s your interest in the case?”

“Mrs. Carmichael’s my client.”

Borman stared at me dumbfounded. “I know confidentiality prevents you from telling me why, but she’s quite the handful, son. Be careful.”

“Yes, sir, I know. And I will. Is there anything you can tell me about her?”

"Not really. The Carmichaels are relatively new to the island. They aren't snowbirds like most residents; they live here year-round, but I don't know them well. As I recall, until Mr. Carmichael's death, we hadn't received any calls from their home or recorded any incidents involving him or his wife."

"Do you know what line of business Carmichael was in?"

"I think he retired from manufacturing somewhere in the Midwest. Ohio, I think. He was considerably older than his wife by about twenty-five years."

"Hmm. Curious."

Borman cleared his throat. "Listen, Drake, widow Carmichael is a voluptuous woman who can wrap a man around her little finger with minimal effort. But you already know that, don't you?"

I looked Borman straight in the eye. "Let's put it this way, Chief. She tried, but I don't entwine easily."

"Good. Keep it that way. Anything else I can do for you?"

"There is one other thing. Have you ever heard Mrs. Carmichael's name referred to as Della Smith, Della Brown, or Della Warren?"

Borman's brows knitted together. "Aliases?"

"The Della Warren may be legit. I think she was married before Carmichael, but I'm unsure of the other names—Smith and Brown."

"Let me see what I can find out. Anything else?"

"No, sir, except for my sincere condolences on the passing of your wife last year. I sent a card but wanted to tell you in person."

"That's kind of you, Drake." A glint of a tear formed in Borman's eyes.

"Well, I appreciate your time, Chief." I rose. So did Borman.

"Don't be a stranger, Drake. It's been good to see you. I'll give you a call when I have more information. When your parents get back, tell them we need to get together." Borman slapped me on the back and walked me out of the station.

~~~

I got home around 12:30 p.m. and had just enough time to jump in the pool for a short swim before I showered and changed for my appointment with Della. Of course, I'd carefully scrutinize the patio and the street before I dove in to make sure Bluto wasn't anywhere around.

Passing in front of the mirror before heading to the pool, I noticed several bruises on my shoulders. Looking more closely, I realized that's where the edge of the skimmer had landed when Bluto pinned me in the pool with the apparatus earlier this morning. Touching the discolorations, I winced at the tenderness. Could these have been the same type of injuries Carmichael had?

I grabbed my Kodak box camera and took several photos of the marks using the mirror's reflection. I also took the camera to the pool and snapped pictures of the skimmer, including the frame. Perching the end of the pole on the ficus hedge, I tried to get several photos of what the skimmer looked like when placed over my head and resting on my shoulders. Of course, I wouldn't know if the camera caught everything until I saw the pictures. If the bruises appeared in the images, maybe Borman could match them to those on Stanley Carmichael. If so, he might have the 'how' of Carmichael's death, but he'd still need the who and why. After my investigation, he might have that, too.

I re-wound the film in my camera, withdrew the roll, and placed it in the envelope to mail to Kodak for
~~~

development. After my swim, I dressed and headed out with Marvin, a Colt Detective Special .38 with a checkered walnut grip, tucked snuggly in my shoulder holster.

CHAPTER 12

I got to Woolworths at about 1:45 p.m. The lunch crowd was thinning out, but lingering customers sat at the lunch counter and in most booths. I found an empty cubicle in the corner and made a beeline toward it. I figured the location would be discrete enough for my meeting with Della.

Irma, the gray-haired waitress I had encountered on my earlier visit, came to the table as soon as I was seated. Without looking up, she flipped open her pad, pulled the pencil from behind her ear, and got ready to take my order.

"What'll you have?"

"Coffee and egg salad sandwich." I hoped to finish by the time Della arrived.

"White or rye?

"Rye."

"Toast the bread?" she asked.

"Sure," I said, handing her the menu.

Accepting it, Irma finally looked up. "Oh, it's you. Here to see Constance?"

"I'm meeting someone, but hope to see Constance before I leave."

"I'll tell her you're here." Irma gave me a half smile before leaving.

I scanned the comings and goings of the customers, looking for Della in case she was early. Irma walked out of the kitchen, engaged Constance in a short conversation behind the counter, and gestured toward my booth. I caught Constance's eye and gave her a slight nod. She smiled. As before, my heart began to race.

In no time, Irma returned with my coffee and sandwich.

"Anything else I can get you?" she asked.

"I may want desert when I'm through," I said.

"Uh-huh, and I know just what kind of dessert you want, too," she said, cocking her head toward Constance. "You hurt that girl, and the wrath of Hercules will come down on you."

"Hercules?"

"Yeah, Smitty, the cook. He's taken quite a shine to her. Not romantically, of course. The man's twice her age. More like a father."

I cleared my throat. Just someone nicknamed after the physically powerful Greek God was enough to give a prospective suitor pause. "I'll keep that in mind."

"You do that," said Irma as she left.

Hastily eating my food, I scanned the restaurant for Della while keeping one eye on Constance as she served customers at the counter. She'd gaze at me occasionally; we'd both smile. When I finished eating, Irma cleared the table and left a check.

My watch showed 2:00 p.m.

No Della.

Dad adhered to a policy regarding tardy clients—"Wait twenty minutes. If they don't show, you're free to move on."

I waited. Five, ten, fifteen minutes. With each glance at my watch, my annoyance level escalated. At twenty minutes after two, still no Della. My irritation was at the point of Vesuvius when Constance approached the table.

"Mr. Marlow?" Her eyes sparkled, as did her smile.

"I was just leaving," I said curtly. Though I wanted to see Constance, a bright spot in an otherwise disappointing afternoon, I wasn't in the mood after being stood up by Della.

"I see. It's just that I was asked to give you something." Constance slipped her hand into the pocket of her smock and withdrew a white envelope. She handed it to me.

"What's this?" I turned the envelope over. My name was written on the front, but there was no return name or address.

"It's from Della."

"She was here?" I catapulted from my seat, my gaze probing the diner.

"She came by earlier today. Seeing her after all these years was wonderful, but she only stayed a few minutes."

"Why didn't you give me the envelope earlier? When I came in?"

"I have a job, Mr. Marlow, and was busy with customers. Della asked me to give you the envelope. Now I have." Constance turned on her heels.

"Wait!" I called, restraining her.

She looked down at my hand on her arm, then at me, her eyes filled with tears.

"Take your hand off her!" A stocky man, with eyes as hard as stone and muscles bulging under a stained cook's apron, stood with his legs apart and arms crossed over his chest. Jutting from his chunky fist was a meat cleaver. Remnants of blood and grist still clung to the blade.

I gulped and immediately withdrew my hand.

"It's alright, Smitty. He didn't hurt me." Constance spoke soothingly and gently touched Smitty's arm as she walked past him.

He gave me a parting scowl punctuated by a growl, turned, and followed her. They both slipped through the swinging door into the kitchen.

My feet seemed glued to the floor while my legs felt like overcooked noodles. My mind whirled in confusion as I let out a huge sigh. I'd just encountered for the second time the one person who could brighten my day. And how did I react? I was so caught up in Della's rudeness in standing me up that I let her go.

Blinking back to reality, I walked out of the diner needing a stiff drink and a quiet place to reflect on my emotions and what had happened. I also wanted to read Della's note, and plan my next move. Smuggler's Cove, a concealed inlet off the Intracoastal that rumrunners used to offload liquor at night, seemed the ideal spot. During daylight hours, the place would be quiet and deserted.

Celia and I headed North on US1. I drove for about twenty minutes, then took a right onto a coral rock road, more like a path, with no name. After another couple of miles, I hit a turnoff to the south. The road curved until it ended at a concealed parking area of hard-packed sand. I backed Celia in behind a hedge of trees and scrub.

Smugglers had carved the secret rendezvous spot out of mangroves and underbrush along the Intracoastal, the site becoming a transfer point for illegal booze that began its run into the U.S. from the Bahamas. Distilleries in Britain, Cuba, and Jamaica shipped the alcohol to Nassau. Others loaded the cases onto schooners and sailed up the east coast of Florida. Smaller contact boats offloaded the liquor at sea and moved the spirits into Florida's canals and coves along the coast for trucks to transport the liquor inland for disbursement.

Cookie had brought me here several months ago when I accompanied him one morning before sunrise to pick up hard liquor, wine, and cordials he clandestinely served to his patrons at the Green Turtle—one of the reasons he could attract so many customers out of season.

I transferred my flask to my pants pocket, removed my jacket, and placed it into the car. Walking about twenty yards, I sat on a primitive bench hewn of oak under a canopy of shade trees and watched the water lazily lap the shore about forty feet away. Turning my face upward, I felt the sea breeze filter through the trees.

This had been some day, I mused. Today started with my assault and progressed with a no-show by my client. As if that wasn't bad enough, the afternoon climaxed with a threat from a man nicknamed Hercules holding a meat cleaver, and I'd driven away the one person I wanted to get to know better. What else could go wrong?

Reaching into my pants pocket, I withdrew my flask of whiskey and raised it to my lips. I took a large swig, as if that would make things all better. I knew it wouldn't, but what it would do was uncoil this tightly wound private investigator. As I sat there, waiting for the liquor to bathe me in a warm glow, I realized that at least something positive had come out of the day. I discovered how Stanley Carmichael may have died—someone put a skimming net over his head and held him under the water until he drowned.

I raised my flask again.

My first inclination was to accuse Bluto, but I had no proof he'd killed Stanley Carmichael except that he'd tried the same thing with me. That's circumstantial evidence, not proof, though the behavior indicated a pattern.

I'd need more evidence to make that allegation stick. But then, I had to remind myself Della hadn't paid me to find out who killed her husband. She'd paid me to find out who she was. Stanley's murderer and Della's identity were exclusive of each other, weren't they? Or were they somehow intertwined—find the killer, find Della's identity? I shook my head. How would that make any sense?

Once again, I raised the flask and swallowed the amber liquid.

"Aaauugghh!" I screamed, my anguished cry swallowed by the underbrush. I was driving myself crazy with questions but no answers.

Then I remembered Della's note. I pulled the crumpled envelope from my pocket and smoothed it, inspecting the handwriting in the dappled light from the trees. The delicate cursive appeared to be made by a woman.

My hand trembled as I slipped my index finger beneath the flap and carefully unsealed the envelope. Inside was a white card. An embossed "D," I assumed for Della, stood out in relief on the front. Gold foil outlined the character, while tiny daisy-like flowers in multiple colors—pink, white, yellow, and purple—embellished the inside raised portion of the "D."

I flipped the card open. Five one hundred dollar bills fluttered out. I gathered the cash and stuffed it into my breast pocket. Then I read Della's note:

Dear Mr. Marlow,
I'm sorry I was unable to meet you. Something came up that needed my attention. I'll be away for a while, but please continue working on my case. I've included additional

money to cover your time and expenses. I'll be in touch.
Della

I rested my head against the tree, downed the last mouthful of whiskey, and closed my eyes.

CHAPTER 13

The sound of muted voices woke me. Orienting myself to my surroundings, I still sat against the tree, my flask and Della's note on my lap, yet I had no idea how long I'd been there. Pitch darkness surrounded me, except for light from a lantern hanging off the front of an approaching vessel where the voices were coming from.

Smugglers!

Beads of sweat broke out on my forehead, and my heart lept to my throat. I needed to get out of there before they saw me and thought I was a spy for the Feds or their trucks arrived to transport the smuggled booze inland. I patted my holster relieved Marvin was still there, but I would use him only as a last resort.

Believing I had enough time to escape before being spotted, I hunched over and groped toward Celia. Just as I got into her front seat, the smugglers pulled ashore. If I started Celia's engine, I knew they'd find me. I had no alternative but to stay put and wait for an opportunity to escape.

The smugglers took hours to offload their cargo by lantern light. All the while, I kept an eye on them through the underbrush. When they stacked the last case, they leisurely smoked several cigarettes. I could hear only snippets of their conversation, but what I heard shook me to the core—the trucks were coming to pick up the liquor. When the drivers pulled their vehicles into the parking area, they would see me. I was now a sitting duck with no option.

I had to get out of there.

Now!

My hand shook as I fingered my keyring and inserted the car key into the ignition. I started Celia's engine and flipped on the headlights. Thankfully, they shone toward the exit, not the smugglers, yet as I put the car in gear, I heard several sharp cracks of a gun. A bullet whizzed over my head, and then I heard a thud. Gunning the engine, I lurched out of Smuggler's Cove and down the winding coral rock road as fast as I could until I reached the highway. Just as I pulled out, three pickup trucks passed me. Gazing in the rearview mirror, I watched their taillights disappear down the road with no name.

I'd escaped in the nick of time.

Maintaining a heavy foot, I drove home as the sun climbed above the horizon. Usually, I'd have enjoyed the sunrise with its splashes of pinks, golds, grays, and blues. This morning, though, I could only stay focused on getting home in one piece. When I reached the cottage, I grabbed my jacket and rounded the car. That's when I saw the wound in Celia's front passenger door.

Inspecting the blemish more closely, I noticed an indentation the size of a quarter marred Celia's black paint. In the center of the dent was a small hole. One of the rumrunner's bullets had penetrated her skin. Opening the door, I searched inside but found no exit hole. Thankfully, the bullet hadn't pierced the interior, but how would I explain the wound at the body shop?

Exhausted from no sleep, the stress of encountering the smugglers, and realizing I could have been killed, I unlocked the cottage door and fell into bed without undressing.

~~~

The jangle of the phone jolted me awake. I grabbed for the handset but knocked it off its cradle and onto the floor. Able to locate the receiver in my half-awake state, I announced, "Marlow," in a groggy voice.

"Thank heaven you're safe. I could strangle you for not calling me yesterday. I've been frantic with worry." Betty Lou's voice pounded in my ears.

"I'm fine," I said, realizing I had a doozy of a headache.

"You don't sound fine. What happened?"

"I'll tell you when I get in."

"You'd better make it snappy. You have a client coming in at 10:15 a.m."

"What time is it?"

"Nine forty-five."

I needed two aspirin, a cold shower, a shave, and a change of clothes to pump new life into my body. Unfortunately, I only had time for the aspirin, a perfunctory shave, and the smoothing of my shirt. My jacket would cover any egregious wrinkles. As bright-eyed and bushy-tailed as I could be from an energy-depleted body that lacked adequate sleep and fuel, I arrived at the office on time and greeted my potential client, Mr. Phillips.

"You've got to find her," he said, entering my office panicked and pacing the room.

"Who?" I asked.
~~~

"My daughter. She's only seventeen. She's run away with one of them scallywag polo players from New Jersey. Her clothes and a suitcase are gone. There's money missing from my wallet. Her mother's frantic with worry." The man, who looked as disheveled as I felt and must have had about as bad a morning as I had a night, paced the room, drawing his fingers through his hair.

"Let's start at the beginning, Mr. Phillips. First, please sit down. What's your daughter's name?" We both sat. I took notes while Mr. Phillips, knees bouncing, answered my questions.

"Priscilla."

"When did you discover she was gone?"

"This morning."

"Did you check with her friends?"

"Her mother called them. No one has seen her."

And so the conversation went. Mr. Phillips hadn't gone to the police because the cut-off age for runaways was sixteen. Having just turned seventeen, Priscilla was old enough to run away voluntarily. But her father knew his daughter had made a terrible mistake; he wanted her back home.

He handed me a photo of Priscilla and a list with as many names of her friends as he and his wife could remember. He also supplied a timeline of her recent activities and information regarding her association with polo players, which was minimal. Before meeting me, he'd already shown his daughter's picture to the ticket clerks at the bus and train stations. Neither had seen her.

For a reasonable retainer, I would start making inquiries and agreed to dig around locally to see what I could turn up before fully committing to the case. Mr. Phillips left satisfied with the arrangements.

My first reaction to Mr. Phillips' premise that his daughter had run off with a polo player left a curious question. With Palm Beach being Florida's *Winter* Polo Capital, with players usually staying just through the season—January through April—what was a polo player doing here in the dead of summer?

I didn't have adequate time to mull that over because as soon as Mr. Phillips left, Betty Lou rushed my office and dropped into a chair.

"Okay, spill the beans," she said, gazing at me with high expectations.

"I haven't even had my morning coffee," I whined.

"That's because it's almost noon. You missed morning." Betty Lou gave me a scornful smile and rose to bring me coffee. "So?" she asked when she returned. She set the mug on the desk and sat back, waiting for me to begin.

"Mr. Phillips wants me to find his missing daughter." I took a sip from my mug.

"Not those beans, silly. I want the beans from yesterday." She placed her elbows on my desk and her chin in her hands. She stared at me.

I told her the whole shebang, from my arrival at the diner, my departure from Smuggler's Cove, and the discovery of the bullet hole.

Betty Lou's eyes bulged as her hand thumped against her chest. "Oh, good Lord! You could have been killed!" Tears pricked her eyes.

"But thankfully, I made it back in one piece." I gave Betty Lou a half smile.

She took in a breath and let it out slowly. "Promise me you won't go back to that place." Her stern eyes pierced mine.

My hands shot up in surrender. "I have no intention of doing so."

“Good. If you hand me Della’s note, I’ll put it into her case file.” Betty Lou extended her palm.

I dug into the pockets of my jacket, pants, and shirt. The cash was still there, but no envelope.

“I’ll be right back,” I said, dashing out the door.

When I got to Celia, I scoured the car—glove compartment, side pockets, floor, and back seat. Still no envelope. The note itself wasn’t that important, I knew what it said, but Della had addressed the envelope to me personally. If the smugglers found that and the card, they would know a Mr. Drake T. Marlow had been at Smuggler’s Cove. Would they think I’d run squealing to authorities to reveal their secret transfer point? Would they hunt me down to shut me up? I’d already had one encounter with a thug. I certainly didn’t want another.

I returned to the office out of breath and discouraged. “The note’s gone along with my monogrammed flask. I must have dropped them when I crept to the car.”

“Well, that’s disappointing. Now—what are you going to do about Constance?”

“Constance?” I was confused by the abrupt change of topic.

“Yeah. You know, the woman you wanted to get to know better but were rude to?”

I gazed incredulously at Betty Lou, then stomped around my office, hands waving in the air. “A brute tried to kill me. My client stood me up. Hercules threatened me. I lost the silver flask my father gave me and Della’s note. And rumrunners now know my name. All that, and you’re more interested in knowing what I intend to do about Constance?” I stopped my raving and stood red-faced, hands on hips, glaring at Betty Lou.

"Gee, Boss. I didn't think about it that way. I was looking out more for your romantic interests—your heart."

"With little concern for the rest of my wellbeing. Out!" My face burned as I pointed to the door.

"Okay, okay. I might have been a bit insensitive." Betty Lou stood and backed toward the open door.

"OUT!"

She turned and hustled from the office, the door banging shut behind her.

I took several deep breaths, trying to calm myself. I needed more sleep, a clean body, fresh clothes, and food. Only then could I think straight instead of running on sheer adrenaline and raw emotion.

Betty Lou gave me a sheepish look and half wave as I stormed out of the office. When I arrived home, I dragged myself to the cottage, looking forward to a prolonged nap. As I reached the door, I stopped dead. On the stoop was my silver flask sitting atop Della's crumpled note.

The smugglers had returned them.

They knew who I was!

Where I lived!

A shiver ran through me, and my heart jumped to my throat as I looked around to see if one of them was hiding somewhere. Not seeing anyone, I retrieved the flask and Della's note. Underneath, a second note emerged. Scribbled in pencil on a scrap of well-creased paper, it read:

> *You dropped these. A gift is under the hedge. I assured everyone you wouldn't squeal.*

There was no signature, only a simple line drawing of a sea turtle—Cookie!

The sun glistened off something to my right. Upon further inspection, I pulled a fifth of Haig & Mactavish whiskey from the bushes. Since Prohibition began a dozen years ago, the British distillery had shipped boatloads of the stuff into Nassau.

Looking at the bottle, I let out a hearty laugh, the expulsion satisfying the need to release the pent-up tension I'd had since yesterday. And then there was the liquor. My flask was empty, but not for long.

I was grateful Cookie had intervened on my behalf. Later tonight, I'd visit the Green Turtle and thank him properly. Right now, though, I desperately needed food, a shower, a nip or two, and to hit the hay. I prayed the phone wouldn't ring and no one would knock on my door while I slept.

CHAPTER 14

The clock showed 7:30 p.m. when I awoke. Knowing Cookie would be serving the final meals of the night and I could catch him for some private conversation, I quickly showered, dressed, and headed to the Green Turtle. I found a table, ordered fried turtle steak, and asked my waitress Angie to tell Cookie I was there.

My meal, as usual, was delicious. The steak, perfectly cooked in a lightly seasoned batter, tasted between fish and beef. The meat wasn't tough but had a firmer quality than fish. Accompanying the meat was a salad, green beans, baked potato, and rolls. The food was just what I needed to perk me up.

After Angie cleared the table and I paid my bill, Cookie came by and sat. He looked around furtively, then leaned in.

"What were you doin' at Smuggler's Cove?" His voice was low yet firm.

I told him about my botched meeting with Della, why I wound up at the cove, and how I almost had two heart attacks that night. The first was when the smugglers' bullets whistled over my head and one hit my car, and the second was when I saw the flask and note on my doorstep.

"Thanks for sticking up for me." I put my hand on Cookie's shoulder and squeezed. "I owe you."

"I was happy to do it, mate, but you might not be so lucky next time. My advice? Stay out of Smuggler's Cove." Cookie regarded me with an unwavering stare.

"Right. That's my last visit." I made an X over my heart and lifted my palm in a swear.

"So, have you discovered who Della is?" asked Cookie.

"No, but I've found she's had more than two names. More like four, to be exact. Ever hear of her being called Della Brown or Della Warren?"

Cookie shook his head.

"Did you know she'd been married before?"

Once again, Cookie shook his head. Tears welled in his eyes.

"Well, that's all I have right now, but I'm still looking into it." While Cookie and I were good friends, I didn't tell him everything about my investigations, especially this one, because he'd had a relationship with Della. The almost falling tears told me he still harbored deep feelings for her.

"Well, let me know if I can help you further." Cookie got up to leave.

"Hey, what do you know about polo players?" I stood, and we walked to the door.

"They come in here durin' polo season for dinner. Have quite the followin', and I've heard they've broken a few hearts around town."

"Do you see them here during the summer?"

"Not usually. The players only stay a few months in the winter. A new case?" Cookie asked.

"Maybe. I'm just looking around to see what turns up. See you later." Cookie and I shook hands, and I returned home. I needed to jot down a few notes so Betty Lou could start making phone calls tomorrow in Mr. Phillips' missing daughter case. I also wanted to scribble down a reminder to myself to mail the film to Kodak for development.

~~~

Betty Lou was making coffee when I arrived at the office the following morning.

"Get a good night's sleep?" she asked with enthusiasm and a smile. Her perky greeting made me believe she'd put our tiff from yesterday behind her.

"Good enough," I said, smiling back at her.

"Great, 'cause you have a busy day ahead of you."

"Oh?" I entered my office to find two typed lists of names, phone numbers, and addresses on my desk. What's this?" I asked Betty Lou, who had followed me into the office.

"While you were out yesterday, Chief Borman called. The first list includes the names of the three friends Della was out with when her husband died. I've included their phone numbers and addresses as I'm sure you'll want to contact each."

"And the second list?" I switched pages.

"It's from the list Mr. Phillips gave you—names, phone numbers, and addresses of Priscilla's friends. I called each to see if they were in town or on summer vacation. I've marked the ones who are here and who I couldn't reach." Betty Lou leaned over the desk and pointed at the list and her markings—"H" for here, "CR" for couldn't reach.

"I'm impressed," I said.

"Also, Constance called."
~~~

I jerked up in surprise.

"When she found out you weren't here, she left a message that she wanted to apologize for what happened at the diner. I got the impression she wants to see you again."

I could barely speak. "Uh, maybe I'll drop by the diner for a late lunch after I've completed some of these interviews." I smiled at Betty Lou.

"I'm sure Constance would appreciate it. Anything else I can do for you, Boss?"

"Didn't I see you making coffee?"

"Of course. Coming right up." Betty Lou scurried from the office and returned moments later, setting a coffee mug before me. "Here you are. One sugar and a dab of milk."

"Thanks. Oh, I almost forgot. Please mail this film to Kodak for development." I handed Betty Lou the small yellow and black pre-addressed envelope containing my film roll.

She dangled the package between her thumb and forefinger. "Important photos?"

"Very," I said.

"If it concerns one of your cases, I suggest you use Dan Stills. He's a professional photographer, develops his own film, and is very discrete. He doesn't develop pictures for everyone, but your father defended him once, and he felt indebted, so he developed films for your father several times. I'm sure he'd accommodate you if I explained we're now working together. Shall I phone him?"

Thankfully, Betty Lou's years working at my father's law firm allowed her to know just about everyone in town, and that information came in handy on multitudes of occasions—like now.

"Would appreciate that very much. Now skedaddle so I can get some work done." I smiled as I glibly shooed her out of my office.

Withdrawing a map of the Palm Beaches from my desk, I spread it out on top, and made a dot on the streets representing each address from Betty Lou's list. Between sips of coffee, I planned my route to save time. First, I'd visit the ladies in Palm Beach regarding Della. After that, I'd drop off the film at Stills' studio, have that late lunch at Woolworths, and work my way across West Palm Beach, where I'd speak with Priscilla's friends.

Betty Lou was right. This was going to be a busy day.

~~~

In the past, when I investigated human or business relationships and wanted to know the real scoop, I worked my way into the inner circle by starting on the outside—the little guy at the bottom, the sometime friend, acquaintance, janitor, receptionist, or mail room clerk. The farther away from the top the person was, the more truth surfaced. The closer the friendship or business associate, the more reluctance there was. As a trained listener, I learned how to read between the lines. And most times, what a person didn't say was as or more important than what they did say.

My first stop was the home of Mrs. Crawford. I knew I needed to be careful about how I presented my questions. I didn't want her to think I was trying to determine if Della was involved in her husband's death, though that was a secondary motive. My hat dangled in my hand as I knocked on the door.

"Just a minute," called a woman's voice before opening the door. "Well, who do we have here?" Her persimmon lips widened into a broad smile as she gave me the once-over.
~~~

"Mrs. Crawford, I'm Drake Marlow, a private investigator." I handed Mrs. Crawford my card.

"And a handsome investigator at that. Come in." Mrs. Crawford stepped back so I could enter. I followed her to the living room.

"Please have a seat. Coffee?" she asked.

"Only if it's already made. I wouldn't want you to go to any trouble."

"I just made a fresh pot. I'll be just a minute." Mrs. Crawford got up and went to the kitchen, allowing me to look around.

Her home was a bungalow similar to Della's and nicely furnished in large mahogany- pieces. The place was a little stuffy to suit my tastes since I liked things more spacious, but to each his own, as the case may be.

"Here we are." Mrs. Crawford brought in a tray laden with two cups of coffee, sugar, cream, napkins, and a plate of scones. She set it on the coffee table and sat next to me. "Help yourself."

"Thank you." I colored my coffee with sugar and cream and took a sip. "Mrs. Crawford—"

"Mavis." Mrs. Crawford placed her hand on my arm. Her touch lingered. "Call me Mavis."

"Alright, Mavis. Mrs. Carmichael has engaged my services, and although I can't tell you the nature of those services, I would like to ask you some questions." I took out my pad and fountain pen for notes.

"Sure. Anything for Della." Mavis's green eyes stood out against the brown curls that framed her tanned face.

"How long have you known Della?"

"About three years, I think."

"So you knew her before she married Stanley."

"Oh, yes. We're good friends."

"Then you'll recall her maiden name before she married." I poised my pen, anxious to write down her answer.

Mavis hesitated. "Funny you should ask; I simply can't recall. She's always been just Della to me, and then Della Carmichael when she married." Mavis's hand trembled as her fingers brought the coffee cup to her lips.

"Did you and your husband attend Della and Stanley's wedding?" I noticed her wedding ring had quite the rock.

"My husband? No, no. I'm a widow. My husband died several years ago."

Yet she still wears her wedding ring?

"So you went to the Carmichaels' wedding alone?"

Mavis cocked her head to the side. "I believe I was out of town now that you mentioned it."

"How often do you spend time with Della?"

"Oh, several times a week, I would think. To go shopping, to the movie, playing bridge, or out to eat."

"You were with Della, Mrs. Jan Carrington, and Mrs. Stella Barnes the afternoon Della's husband died, correct?"

"What a tragic day!" She feigned a tear at the corner of her eye and caught it with her napkin.

"Can you tell me what the three of you ladies did that day?"

Mavis looked at her watch. "Oh, dear. I didn't realize the time. I'm going to be late for my appointment. I hope you'll excuse me, but I must go. It was nice meeting you, Mr. Marlow." She stood and held out her hand. Her fingers reeked of nervous moisture.

I gathered my things, and Mavis saw me to the door. I knew she lied about not knowing Della's maiden name, but I knew I wouldn't get much more out of her even with a second try. A cover-up was in the wind, and I craved to know what it was all about.

As I pulled out from Mavis's home, a curtain fluttered in the front window as she tried to hide behind it. I figured she was already phoning Jan Carrington and Stella Barnes to alert them of my visit. I still planned to call on them, hoping to obtain some information, but intuition told me not to be optimistic.

As suspected, Jan Carrington wasn't home; neither was Stella Barnes. I'd try again, next time unannounced by Mavis. Thwarted from my planned interviews, I drove over the bridge into West Palm Beach and dropped off my roll of film at Stills Professional Photographer. The photos would be ready in a week, and I hoped they'd prove my theory—that Stanley Carmichael's bruises matched mine, and he'd been assaulted with a similar device and in a like manner. Maybe he'd even died from being held underwater by the skimmer. And maybe "Bluto" was the one holding onto the other end. Then again, perhaps it was someone else. But who?

Chapter 15

Since it was still too early for a late lunch, I decided to stop at Judy Palmer's house. She was a friend of Priscilla's but not her best friend or a member of her inner circle. She was one of those in the outer circle who I hoped would give me straight answers.

"A polo player?" asked Judy in a soft tone of disbelief. The high school junior—thin with light brown curly hair and brown eyes—sat in her living room on the couch. I sat in a side chair while Judy's mother sat in another.

"That's what her father believes," I said.

"I don't see how that could be, Mr. Marlow. Polo is for the wealthy Palm Beach crowd. Where would Priscilla get the money for a ticket to the match or the clothes and hat she would wear? And how would she get out to the polo fields?"

"If a polo player didn't lure her off, what might have happened?"

"Umm, have you talked to Tom Brannigan? I believe they were good friends. Maybe more."

"He's on my list, but you're the first of Priscilla's friends I've spoken to. Please tell me what you know about Tom and Priscilla. Her parents are frantic to find her, as I'm sure your parents would be if you left without telling them."

"Well—" Judy looked at her mother for reassurance. She nodded. "I don't know anything for sure, mind you, but I've seen them together on several occasions. They seemed quite—chummy."

"Chummy?"

"I saw them kiss once behind the bleachers."

"Do you think they would run off together?"

Judy shrugged.

"Anything else you can tell me? Even little details could be important." I held Judy's gaze.

"That's about all I can tell you, Mr. Marlow. I like Priscilla, but we're not that close. Perhaps one of her closer friends can give you more information."

"I understand. Just one more question, Judy. Who was Priscilla's best friend?" I had spoken to the outer circle, now I needed to head to the interior. But first, I needed to know who was at the top of the list.

"That would be Leslie Anne Carson. They were inseparable." Judy raised her hand, her middle and index fingers crossed, indicating a tight relationship.

"Thank you for your time," I said before leaving. "And please keep this conversation private. Do I have your word?" I gave Judy a stern eye.

She nodded.

I had the name Tom Brannigan on my list, but Mr. Phillips didn't emphasize his name or say anything about his romantic relationship with Priscilla. Yet, I didn't want to be dismissive of information that seemed genuine. I made his home my next stop.

"Tom isn't home," Mrs. Brannigan quietly said after I introduced myself. She stood on the front porch of her middle-class clapboard home on Collier Street, her brow puckered and her arms hugging her chest.

"If you can tell me where he is, I'll gladly drive over to see him. This is important."

"I—I don't know where he is, Mr. Marlow. His father and I found his bed empty early this morning." She stood on tiptoes, eyes darting over my shoulders as if she were looking for her son to reappear at any moment.

"Could he be with Priscilla Phillips?"

"Priscilla Phillips! That tramp? Why would he be with her?" Mrs. Brannigan's eyes turned ice cold.

"Mrs. Brannigan, Priscilla Phillips is missing, just like your son. Her father has engaged my services to try to find her. One of your son's classmates told me that Tom and Priscilla may have had a romantic attraction."

"He's my only son," said Mrs. Brannigan, her voice breaking. Her shoulders drooped, and her gaze turned downward. A sniffle escaped as she brought her hands to her face. Suddenly, her shoulders shook, and her snivel turned into uncontrollable sobbing. Tears ran down her cheeks and dripped off her chin.

I reluctantly positioned my arm around her shoulders. "Mrs. Brannigan, would you like to sit down?"

She nodded, hands still covering her face.

I led her to a rattan settee on the porch and handed her my handkerchief. I sat in an adjacent white wooden rocker, waiting for her to regain her composure. Not having children, I couldn't imagine how painful it would be to have a child run away. Having witnessed how distraught Mr. Phillips was yesterday and Mrs. Brannigan was today, I hoped Priscilla and Tom were safe and this investigation would have a positive outcome.

"He left a note," Mrs. Brannigan said, wiping her inflamed and teary eyes.

"May I read it?"

She withdrew a folded, well-worn paper from the pocket of her print dress and handed it to me. From the smeary writing and the paper's dampness, many tears had fallen on the note.

Dear Mom and Dad,

You're wrong about Priscilla. She's a beautiful person, and I love her.

Tom

"Mrs. Brannigan, did you call Tom's friends to see if they'd seen him?" I returned the letter.

Mrs. Brannigan shook her head and put the letter back into her pocket.

"So, no one else knows Tom's missing?" I asked.

"Hank didn't want to make a big issue out of this. He works for the city and felt Tom's running away could be most embarrassing for us. He'd have gone out looking for Tom but had a business meeting this morning. Before he left, he assured me if we gave Tom some space, he'd come home on his own."

"I don't think they've gone far, especially without a car. But they could have taken a bus or train. Do you know where your son might have gone? Maybe to a relative's home?" I withdrew my pad and ink pen to take notes.

Holding the damp handkerchief, Mrs. Bannigan wrung her hands in her lap. "My sister, Margaret Farrington, lives in Orlando."

"Anyone else you can think of?"

"The rest of our relatives live out of state."

"Could you describe Tom—the color of his hair, eyes, height, build? Do you know what he was wearing? Do you have a photo?"

"Tom's about five feet nine, medium build with sandy hair and blue eyes. He took several outfits with him, so I don't know what he's wearing. Wait a minute, and I'll get a photo."

I waited while Mrs. Brannigan went back into the house. Moments later, she handed me a picture of Tom.

"I'm going to recheck the bus and train depots. Mr. Phillips did this yesterday, but perhaps something new will turn up. I'll get back to you when I learn something. Please understand, Mrs. Brannigan, that I must notify Mr. Phillips about Tom and his note." I stood.

"I understand," she said, rising. "Please find them, Mr. Marlow." Her gaze pleaded with me, as did her grasp on my hands.

"I'll do my best, ma'am."

I had just enough time to check the bus and train stations before heading to Woolworths. No one at the train station had seen Tom and Priscilla, but the ticket master at the bus terminal said he thought two young people matching their descriptions bought tickets to Tampa. The bus left at 9:00 a.m. this morning.

Thinking about the timeline, I was hard-pressed to make heads or tails of it. If the bus Priscilla and Tom took didn't depart until this morning, why did Priscilla leave home the day before? And where did she stay the last two nights? My hunch was that one of her friends knew about her rendezvous with Tom and put her up for the two nights. Probably a close, maybe best friend. Someone Priscilla could trust to keep her deepest secrets and lie for her if necessary—Leslie Anne Carlson.

Running on nothing more than the cup of coffee Betty Lou made for me this morning, I was famished and needed sustenance before continuing. Of course, my lunch at Woolworths would serve several purposes—refueling my body, giving me a break from my cases, and seeing Constance again. Afterward, I'd talk to Leslie Anne before returning to the office.

CHAPTER 16

Irma noticed me immediately as I entered the diner and sat at a booth.

She hustled over.

"Good afternoon, Mr. Marlow. I hope we're not going to have a repeat of the other day." She viewed me with a cautious eye.

"I'm not here for that," I said, raising my hands in surrender. "I came in for lunch. That's all."

"In that case, please have a menu. Meatloaf is the special of the day. Comes with mashed potatoes, gravy, green beans, and a roll. What can I get you to drink?"

"Sweet iced tea would be great."

While Irma went to get my tea, I scanned the diner. I saw Constance serving customers behind the counter, but I hadn't yet caught her eye. While I continued gazing in her direction, hoping she'd glance my way, she went through the swinging door into the kitchen instead.

"Drake? Drake Marlow? It's Sam Carlton from high school." Sam slapped his chest and gazed at me in surprised recognition. "For heaven's sake, how are you? It's been a long time." He thrust his hand across the table.

I tried to stand, but the table impeded a complete upright position. "Sam, it's good to see you." I extended my hand. Sam had played first base while I played shortstop for the West Palm Beach Sharks.

"Drake, meet my wife, Annabell." She and I nodded at each other. "Honey, this was the team's most popular and talented player. The stands filled to capacity every Friday night just to see him play. And he didn't disappoint." Sam gave me a wink.

"I think you're overstating a bit. It didn't hurt that we had a winning season," I said.

"I heard you were back in town. Is your wife with you? We'd love for you two to come by the house sometime." Sam raised his brows in expectation.

"It's just me, Sam." I gave him a stiff smile.

"I thought you got married."

"Uh, it didn't work out." This was the first time since I'd been back that anyone had brought up the subject.

"Oh, I'm sorry."

"Look, honey," said Annabell, putting a hand on Sam's arm, "Drake came here for a quiet lunch. Maybe you two can get together and talk another time." Annabell tilted her head to the side; her soft brown eyes gave me an understanding look.

"Sure. Well, it's good to see you again, Drake." Sam gave me a half-wave and left.

I'd been unprepared for this conversation, but I should have expected it at some point. My parents were ecstatic when I told them I was finally getting married and probably told their friends. Few had heard things hadn't worked out, and I hadn't been back long enough to run into anyone that knew.

"Here's your tea," said Irma, setting it down.

"I'll have the special," I said, handing her back the menu.

"It should be out shortly. By the way, I told Constance you're here. She said she'd see you in a few minutes. Her customers are about to leave." Before returning to the kitchen, Irma gave me a wink and a half smile. I took them as a positive sign.

When Constance returned to the counter, she glanced my way and smiled. Funny how her small gesture set my heart racing. I gave her a slight nod and returned the grin, yet anxiety at entertaining a new relationship remained just below the surface. Trust—that's what relationships were based on. Could I trust another woman?

Everything looked and smelled so good when my food arrived that I had to restrain myself from scarfing it down. I was about finished when Constance appeared.

"Hello, Mr. Marlow," she said in her soft voice.

I wiped my mouth and half stood, the table impeding a full stance. "Miss Grimly."

"Please sit and finish your meal. I'm sure your secretary told you, but I wanted you to hear directly from me. I'm sorry for what happened the last time you were here."

"Hercules won't be rushing out with a cleaver again, will he?" I leaned to the side as though I was looking for him.

"No." She giggled. "I talked with him, and he knows he can't do that, especially to someone I like." Constance's cheeks turned as pink as her lipstick.

I sat there, unsure of what to say.

"Well, I just wanted you to know. I'll have Irma bring your ticket." Constance smiled and turned toward the kitchen.

Watching her walk away, I sat mired in a jumble of emotions. Part of me wanted to jump up and stop her. The pain of my past, though, jolted me back to reality. I knew I wasn't over the rejection I'd experienced, nor was I sure I wanted to get involved with another woman. Yet I was drawn to Constance. Would having a cup of coffee and getting to know her better be such a bad thing? By the time I answered that question with a 'no,' she had disappeared behind the swinging door. I settled my bill and then dropped a nickel in the diner pay phone to call Betty Lou.

"It's me," I said.

"Everything okay?"

"Mostly. I need you to make a few phone calls and set up a meeting this evening."

"Sure. Who do you want included?"

"Call Mr. Hank Brannigan, who works for the city of West Palm Beach, and Mr. Phillips. Ask them and their wives to meet me at the office at 5:30 p.m. I have an update on Priscilla and Tom."

"Who are Mr. Brannigan and Tom?"

"Sorry, I forgot you don't know. Hank Brannigan is the father of Tom Brannigan. He's the young man who ran off with Priscilla." I knew I didn't have solid proof of this, but my gut told me my suspicion was correct.

"Tom's the polo player?"

"Not exactly. I'll explain everything when I get back to the office. In the meantime, call the families and round up more chairs so everyone, including you, can sit in my office. I'm in West Palm and have one more stop before heading back. I should be there in about an hour."

"You got it."

The drive to Leslie Anne's home took about ten minutes. Her home was about three blocks from Priscilla's house in the same neighborhood. Mrs. Carson—brown eyes set in a heart-shaped face surrounded by brunette waves—answered the door.

"May I help you?"

"Yes, ma'am. I'm Drake Marlow of Marlow Investigations in Palm Beach." I handed her a card. "I'm here to speak with your daughter, Leslie Anne, about her friend, Priscilla Phillips. She's missing."

"Missing? How could she be missing? She was here the last two nights and spends so much time with us that she's like a second daughter. We'd know if she was missing."

Bingo. That was the information I needed. But her statement didn't tell the whole story.

"Priscilla's alright, isn't she?" Concern marked Mrs. Carson's face.

"As far as I know, ma'am."

"Well, please come in, Mr. Marlow, and I'll get Leslie Anne. She's in her room." Mrs. Carson opened the screen door for me to enter. She led me to the living room and offered me a seat while she went upstairs to get Leslie Anne.

Leslie Anne, a petite young woman, had sandy hair drawn back from her face and hung in curls below her shoulders. I stood as she entered the room. She took one look at me, turned abruptly, and started back up the stairs.

"Young lady," said Mrs. Carson, "you come back here right now. Mr. Marlow needs to speak with you about Priscilla."

"Mother, when you said someone was here to see me, I thought it was one of my friends."

"Never you mind about that. Priscilla is missing, and you know something about it. Now get back here and answer Mr. Marlow's questions."

Leslie Anne hesitantly walked back into the living room. We all sat.

"Hello, Leslie Anne, I'm here because Mr. and Mrs. Phillips are worried sick about their missing daughter. I believe you know why she left and where she went. It would be best if you tell me what you know."

Leslie Anne lowered her head and eyeballed her mother, who gave her a stern 'you'd better tell him' look.

"I understand you may think you're ratting on your best friend, but I ask you to consider her parents. They think she ran off with an unknown polo player when she's really with Tom Brannigan."

Leslie Anne sucked air, and her eyes grew wide. "How did you know?"

"It's my job to find the right people and ask the right questions. Now, why did Priscilla spend the night at your house? Why did you lie to her parents when they called to inquire about her whereabouts? And why did Tom and Priscilla head to Tampa?"

Mrs. Carson's eyes narrowed at her daughter. "You knew all about this? I brought you up better than that."

"Yes, ma'am, but you have to understand. Priscilla swore me to secrecy." Tears pooled in the young girl's eyes.

"Well, tell Mr. Marlow what you know. Later, when your father gets home, we'll discuss the consequences of this little stunt."

Leslie Anne folded her hands in her lap. "Mr. Marlow, Priscilla and Tom are in love. Neither of their parents was keen on the relationship, so they kept it secret until they couldn't stand it anymore. They didn't want to sin by—well—you know—so Priscilla left home a day early to throw her parents off. She slept here so she could go with Tom this morning. My parents didn't think anything of her staying because Priscilla always stays overnight. Sorry, Mom."

"And the only way they could convince their parents they were serious was to get married?" I asked.

"They heard there was a chapel in Tampa where they could marry without their parents' consent as long as they were both seventeen. They took the bus there this morning."

Mrs. Carson looked bewildered and speechless.

"I'm meeting both Tom and Priscilla's parents shortly to give them the news. If Tom or Priscilla contact you, please tell them their parents love them very much and want to know they're safe. Ask them to contact their parents as soon as possible."

"Yes, sir."

"Thank you for telling the truth, Leslie Anne. I know it was difficult, but you did the right thing."

By the look on Leslie Anne's face, she wasn't so sure.

"Mrs. Carson, I'm sure you'll want to speak to your daughter, so I'll let myself out." I rose and made my exit.

~~~

Returning to the office, I greeted the Phillips, who had already arrived, then went to my office to gather my thoughts and wait for the Brannigans. Betty Lou showed everyone into my office as soon as they gathered. The couples acknowledged each other in a civil but cool manner. Once we were all seated, I began.

"Thank you for coming to the office on such short notice. I wanted to update you on your children as quickly as possible." From there, I launched into how I became involved, who I spoke to, and what information was forthcoming.
~~~

Everyone was quiet and civil until I got to the part where Tom and Priscilla had traveled by bus to Tampa to get married.

"Married? Priscilla's still a baby! What does she know about being a wife?" Mrs. Phillips choked back tears. Her husband offered his hanky.

"Our Tom was perfectly happy at home. He wouldn't have left unless your daughter used some magical powers to lure him away." Mrs. Brannigan glared at the Phillips.

Mr. Phillips flew to his feet, red-faced. "What do you mean magical powers? Are you insinuating that our Priscilla is a witch?"

Mr. Brannigan jumped up. "My wife's saying if the shoe fits!"

"If the shoe fits? Your Tom lured Priscilla away!" yelled Mrs. Phillips, springing to her feet and pointing an accusing finger at the Brannigans.

"How dare you accuse my son," cried Mrs. Brannigan, hopping up.

Suddenly, the room exploded with expletives and angry faces as the four parents hurled insults and pointed fingers at each other. The cacophony of yelling was ear-splitting.

Betty Lou's expression—wide eyes and open mouth—directed at me conveyed, "Do something!"

I vaulted from my seat, slammed my hands on the desk, glowered at both couples, and yelled, "That's enough!"

The couples shut up, their attention on me.

I took a deep breath. "Getting hostile with each other won't bring your children back or solve anything. For heaven's sake, by now, you're inlaws. Seems like it's more than Tom and Priscilla who need to grow up!" I fisted my hips and sent piercing looks at each parent. "All of you, sit down!" I emphasized my demand with index fingers pointing at their chairs.

The couples gazed at each other, then sat.

I also sat, hoping my blood pressure and heart rate would return to normal.

"Now," I said in a steady and authoritative voice. "I understand why you're upset. I, too, had mixed emotions about Tom and Priscilla. They're so young. Yet, many couples marry in their teens and stay together. Take my parents, for instance. They eloped when they were seventeen, claiming they, too, were hopelessly in love."

All eyes were glued on me, especially Betty Lou's. I continued.

"Dad worked as many as three jobs at a time to support my mother and the two babies that arrived within three years. One of his jobs was cleaning offices at a law firm. When he discovered the law library, he read everything he could get his hands on and discussed the cases with the partners. Recognizing his interest in law and how much he'd absorbed in such a short time, the partners hired him as an assistant and offered to help him get a law degree. He had a very successful law practice, retired recently, and took my mom on a European vacation of a lifetime. My parents have been married for thirty-five years."

I paused for a reaction. No one said a word.

"I'm sharing this with you to provide an optimistic scenario so you can forgive your children, move past your hurt, and embrace the newly married couple. They're going to need your support, not your condemnation. And when they have children, they'll be your grandchildren." I waggled my finger between the couples.

"You're right, of course, Mr. Marlow.." Mrs. Brannigan turned toward the Phillips. "I'm sorry I lost my temper."

"And we apologize for losing ours," said Mr. Phillips.

"Leslie Anne should hear from Priscilla," I assured the group. "So, I've asked her to tell Priscilla both sets of parents love them, are concerned about their safety, and want them to call home as soon as possible. Please let me know if you hear from either of them. Until then, we can do nothing more than pray and wish them the best." I stood, indicating the meeting was over.

After everyone left, Betty Lou and I moved the extra chairs from the office back into the building's storeroom under the stairs.

"I worked for your father for twenty years and never knew your parents eloped or were that young when they married. I thought they met at church after graduating from high school," said Betty Lou, scooting a chair into the storage room.

"It was a crock," I said.

Betty Lou straightened. "What?"

"The story. I made it up. I wanted the couples to take their minds off their situation and hear something positive. It *was* a good story, don't you think?" I winked at Betty Lou.

She scowled at me. Then her lips turned upward, and she broke into uproarious laughter.

I joined her.

"I hope neither couple runs into your parents when they return, or you'll have to make up another story to cover that one. That's what happens with falsehoods, you know. One begets another." Betty Lou clucked her tongue as we walked down the hall and back to the office.

She was right, of course, so there was no need to comment on her pearl of wisdom.

Betty Lou walked to the filing cabinet and withdrew her purse. “Have a good weekend, Boss,” she said, grinning as she left the office.

Now that the office was quiet, I sat at my desk—feet on top, a small glass of whiskey in one hand, a smoke in the other—and figuratively patted myself on the back for discovering the whereabouts of Tom and Priscilla. I truly hoped they’d reconcile with their parents. They would all need each other to make this new marriage work.

The Phillips investigation had only taken a few days, and now that the case was over, I needed to turn my attention back to Della Carmichael. I still needed to find out who she was. The lady had given me quite the mystery, and though I wasn’t sure what my next step would be, tonight I needed a savory dinner and a good night’s sleep. Tomorrow, I’d think about Della and figure out my next move.

CHAPTER 17

Early Saturday morning, I walked the few blocks from my abode to the beach, where I planned to watch the sunrise and do a little swimming and sunning. There wasn't a cloud in the sky except those that formed a rippling dark gray border along the horizon. The water was as tranquil as I'd ever seen—like glass, my dad would say. Seagulls and pelicans glided on a light breeze, and waves lapped lazily at the shore, leaving a meandering ribbon of foam and seaweed. After spreading my blanket and removing my beach jacket and shoes, I walked to the ocean's edge, stepped into the tepid surf, and gazed out over the blue-green water. Not a white cap or boat scratched its surface as far as the eye could see.

Against the vast landscape, I felt like a speck. And yet, my parents and Sunday school teachers taught me each of us is unique and has a purpose. I pondered what mine was. For some reason, this introspection brought me back to Della. Maybe her walking into my office wasn't as random an act as I supposed. Perhaps her arrival in my life was divine providence meant for a bigger purpose. Instead of viewing her as someone whose case would easily pay the rent and keep Betty Lou employed, maybe I needed to see her through a fresh lens.

A tingling sensation began in my toes and swelled through my body as I continued this internal reflection. If Della didn't know who she was, why was that? Goodness knows she'd had enough names, so why didn't she tell me which ones were hers? And why would she take such a drastic measure to expose herself to coerce me into sticking with her case? Sure, she might be used to doing that to get her way, but it seemed extreme, desperate. There had to be a more profound explanation.

When the tingling reached my head, it exploded into the proverbial "lightning strike." Suddenly, I knew what to do. I needed to go back to the beginning—Della's beginning. Where was she born? To whom was she born? Where did she grow up? Who knew her?

Could a medical condition—a severe illness, amnesia, or traumatic event—have caused her memory loss? Maybe she'd been adopted and was given the last name of her adoptive parents and not her birth parents? What if she grew up in an orphanage? What was her name then?

The person who knew Della best—Stanley Carmichael—was dead. But her former lover and roommate were still alive. So were her lady friends and the women who worked with her at the dance hall. Then there was her protector—"Bluto." Collectively, they had to have more pieces to this puzzle than I did.

Standing erect and breathing in the warm, salty air, I vowed to pursue this case until there was nothing left to find. I'd re-interview those who knew Della, and to get to the bottom of this mystery, I'd unleash the most potent weapons I had in my arsenal—Betty Lou and Willie.

CHAPTER 18

"Hey, Boss, have a nice weekend?" Betty Lou bounced into the office and stashed her lunch in the file cabinet.

I rose from my desk and walked to the threshold between our offices. "You won't need that today. I'm taking you out for lunch."

"Oh? To what do I owe this honor?" Betty Lou's wide eyes gazed at me in surprise.

"We need to talk with Constance about Della."

"I thought you already did that?" Betty Lou moved to her desk and sat.

"I did, but I've had a revelation about how to move forward with this investigation, and I'm going to need your help."

"Care to enlighten me?"

I pulled a reception chair close to Betty Lou's desk, leaned in, and told her about my experience at the beach and how I wanted to go back to Della's beginning. "To do that, I need to reinterview everyone I've already spoken with, and I want you to help."

"You mean you're elevating me to investigator?" Betty Lou gave me a broad smile.

"Call it what you like. You're a valued team member with skills I don't possess, and I'd like you to use them."

"So what you're saying is that I'm a woman and can move in circles you can't."

I rolled my eyes. "Yeah. Something like that."

"Well, I'm glad you finally recognize my worth." Betty Lou sat back and gave me a smug grin.

"I'd like you to talk to Della's lady friends and learn all you can about her past."

"And just how am I going to do that?"

"You're a clever investigator. Take this week to see what you can find out. Come and go as you please to the office."

"Who will answer the phone?"

Just then, the telephone rang. Betty Lou raised her brows and nodded at the handset in a "see what I mean" gesture.

I grabbed the phone.

"Marlow Investigations...Yes, this is Drake Marlow...Thanks, Mr. Stills...I'll be by today to pick them up."

"You *can* answer the phone," said Betty Lou.

I ignored her remark. "The photos are ready. We'll pick them up when we go to lunch. In the meantime, I'm going down to talk with Willie and then to the Green Turtle. That should give you time to figure out how to approach the ladies." I winked at Betty Lou as I grabbed my jacket and hat, planted a kiss on the shark's tooth, and made my exit.

As usual, Willie was at his paper stand, passing out the latest news to those entering the Everglades Club.

"Mr. Marlow." Willie nodded as I approached. "Here for your papers?"

I looked around furtively before speaking in a low voice. "That and I have an assignment for you. Can you come to the office so we can talk about it?"

Willie's eyes narrowed, and he cocked his head to the side. "You know I cain't come during the day. Someone might see me. They don't allow coloreds in the Worth Avenue shops." Willie scanned our surroundings as though somebody might be listening.

"Sorry, Willie. I forgot about that. How about tonight after dark? Or, can we meet somewhere?"

"Come to my house about 9:00 p.m. We can talk then."

"Your wife won't mind?"

"She'll understand."

"Great. I'll need your address."

Willie scribbled his address on the edge of the front page of the *Palm Beach Post* and handed me that paper along with the *Miami Herald*. I paid him, and we nodded to each other as I left and walked toward the Green Turtle. I wanted to speak with Cookie again. While he gave me an overall sense of his relationship with Della, I needed to learn more. I entered the kitchen by the back door and found the prep cooks chopping food for the lunch crowd.

"Cookie around?" I asked.

One of the prep cooks pointed his knife down a hallway toward Cookie's office tucked into the corner of the building. I heard him ordering vegetables over the phone as I headed in that direction. He waved as I poked my head in the door and pointed to a chair opposite his desk. I sat and waited until he was free.

"Hello, mate. What brings you 'round this mornin'?" Cookie wore casual clothes covered by a clean apron. Obviously, he hadn't done any prep work yet.

"I'm still working on Della's case and need to ask you some more questions." The way he'd teared up the last time he spoke of her, I was unsure he'd still be amenable to talking.

"I don't know if there's anythin' else to tell." He looked at me with the same love-lorn eyes he'd shown before.

"I must find out who Della is, not for my sake, but for hers."

Cookie leaned forward. "What's the John Dory?"

"John Dory?" I figured that was another Australian phrase I was unfamiliar with.

"The story, mate, the story."

I hesitated, trying to decide what information I should share. But then I figured Cookie might not say anything if I didn't offer a tidbit.

"She's the one that wants to know. That's why she hired me."

Cookie stared at me. He still found talking about Della painful, but I was sure he had answers he didn't even know he had.

"No worries, mate. I'll tell you what I know if it will help her."

"Tell me again how you met."

"Here. At the bar. She was waiting for her girlfriends."

"Do you remember their names?"

Cookie shook his head. "Can't say I do, but they worked at the dance hall with her."

"How did you and Della wind up going out?"

"It was her idea."

"She asked you out? That same night?" I knew Della wasn't the kind of woman who made a move unless she got something for it. I wondered what she got besides the obvious.

"Yeah. I thought it a bit quick myself, but with a Sheila like Della, you don't hesitate." Cookie gave me a sly grin and wiggled his brows.

"I understand. How often did you go out? Where did you go?"

"Oh, I'd say we went out about once a week on my day off. We'd drive down to Ft. Lauderdale or Miami. We never stayed around here except for one time."

"What did you talk about?"

"Mostly, I did the talkin'. She seemed interested in how I became a chef."

"Did she ever mention her childhood, where she was born, her parents, or anything about her background?"

"Hmm. Now that I think about it, she told me very little about herself. She never said where she came from, but I sensed she grew up in Florida but not down here. Every once in a while, she'd say something with a distinct Florida drawl, but it seemed she was trying hard to disguise it."

"You said that one time you and Della stayed around here. What did you do?"

"It was kind of funny. She wanted to know how a chef chops onions without cutting their fingers or crying. I showed her, and then she wanted to try. Unfortunately, she wound up slicing her thumb. I tried to take her to the doctor for stitches, but she refused. When I insisted, she became hysterical and said she hated doctors and would never set foot in another doctor's office or hospital again."

"Curious. What about the cut?" I asked.

"I cleaned the wound with medical spirits and bandaged it the best I could. The next time I saw Della, the cut was healin' nicely. "

"Anything else you can remember about her personal life?"

Cookie thought a moment, then shook his head.

"Well, if you do, please let me know. Even the tiniest detail could be important." I rose to leave.

"Sure, mate," he said, rising.

When I returned to the office, Betty Lou sat hunched over her desk, writing on a notepad.

"Hi, Boss. Learn anything new?" She flipped a few pages and closed the pad.

"As a matter of fact, yes."

"Me, too. Want to rendezvous in your office and compare notes?"

"Ready when you are."

We walked into my office and sat.

"Ladies first," I said, gesturing toward her.

"Okay. First, the bad news. I finally heard back from my contacts regarding 'Bluto.' No one knows him. That means he's from out of town. The good news is they'll keep their eyes peeled now that they know we're asking about him. If he shows up again, we'll hear something."

"What about the ladies? Figured out how to approach them?"

"Still thinking about that, but rest assured, I'll come up with something. Your turn." Betty Lou gazed at me expectantly.

"First, I'm meeting Willie at his home tonight at 9:00 p.m. I have an assignment for him."

"Do you think it's wise to go into Pleasant City? You being white, I'm sure you'll look out of place."

"Willie doesn't live there. He lives in the Freshwater District. I'll still look out of place but don't worry. He wouldn't have asked me to come to his house if it wasn't safe for both of us. I'll be fine."

Betty Lou bit her lip. "I hope so."

"On a different note, Cookie told me some interesting things. He said Della's friends were ladies from the dance hall. I didn't know that. And he said that occasionally she spoke with a distinct Florida accent. I never heard it, but perhaps that will help you. Lastly, he told me Della cut her hand once, and while he tried to take her to the hospital for stitches, she hysterically told him she'd never go to a doctor or hospital again."

"Hmm," said Betty Lou, tapping her cheek with the eraser end of her pencil. "I wonder what that means."

"Just one more scrap of information we'll put in our file. Eventually, it will all add up."

"I'll type that up and add it to the file." Betty Lou grasped a manilla folder from her lap and waggled it at me. By its burgeoning thickness, the case was growing.

I looked at my watch. "I've got to make some calls but be ready at noon. We'll swing by Stills, pick up the photos, and head for Woolworths."

Betty Lou nodded. "See you then, Boss."

~~~

"Ouch!" said Betty Lou, bending down to inspect the bullet hole in Celia's door. "Quite the wound."

"Yeah. I haven't had time to take it to Sonny's Garage for repair." I opened the door for Betty Lou, then circled Celia and slipped behind the wheel.

"That bullet could have hit you." Betty Lou's eyes teared as though the bullet hole punctuated the gravity of that harrowing night.
~~~

"But it didn't," I said soothingly. I placed a hand on hers and squeezed. "Now, let's go get those photos."

I drove to West Palm Beach, picked up the photos at Stills, and stuffed them into my jacket pocket without looking at them. I figured Betty Lou and I could do that over lunch. If they showed what I hoped, we'd drop in and see Borman at the Palm Beach police station on the way back to the office.

Woolworths was busy, but Betty Lou and I were able to grab a vacated booth. As we settled in, we panned the diner. Neither of us saw Irma or Constance. I figured they were in the kitchen and would be out any minute.

A waitress with "Susan" on her name tag came to the table. "Here's our menu and today's specials. May I get you something to drink while you look them over?" Her brunette hair, cut in a bob, bounced as she turned to gaze from me to Betty Lou.

"Sure. I'll have coffee," I said.

"Same for me," said Betty Lou.

"Aren't you Constance's friend?" asked Susan, pointing at me with the end of her pencil.

"Yes," I said, my face flushing.

"Well, I'll be back in a jiffy with the coffees." Susan smiled and turned toward the counter.

"Seems like you've made an impression on the Woolworth waitresses." Betty Lou gave me her crooked grin.

"I guess. What are you having?" I scanned the menu but returned to today's special—spaghetti, meat sauce, a side salad, and garlic toast.

"That special looks awfully good. Much better than my cold toasted cheese sandwich in the file cabinet." Betty Lou let out a chuckle.

Susan returned with our coffees. “Have you decided?” she asked.

“We’ll have two specials,” I said, handing her the menus.

“Very good. I’ll be back in a jiffy.”

“Seems like the word of the day is ‘jiffy,’” said Betty Lou once Susan was out of earshot.

“I haven’t seen Constance, have you?” For the third time, I searched the diner for her.

“No, but maybe it’s her day off?”

“She’s off on the weekends. She should be here today. Do you mind asking Susan for her when she brings our lunch?”

“What’s the matter? Don’t want to look interested?”

I scowled at Betty Lou. “In the meantime, these photos are burning a hole in my pocket. Let’s look at them.” I pulled the packet from my jacket and opened the flap.

“You take a look, Boss, then pass them to me.”

One after another, I gazed at the photos of my shoulder bruises and reenactment of the assault. When through, I passed the images on to Betty Lou.

“Chief Borman said that Stanley Charmichael had small rectangular bruises on his shoulders.” I pointed to the photos of my bruises and the one with the skimmer resting on my shoulders.

“Bluto? He killed Stanley Carmichael in the same way he assaulted you?”

“Entirely possible. We need to get these photos to Borman, so he can start looking for the big guy. Of course, I’ll probably need to file a police report on my assault so he can tie the two incidents together.” I gathered the photos and returned the packet to my jacket pocket.

“Here ya go. Two lunch specials.” Susan set plates in front of us. “Can I warm up your coffee?”

"Please," said Betty Lou. "I haven't seen Constance. Is she working today?"

"She's home. I believe she's got a cold, but she should be in tomorrow. Did you want to leave her a message?"

"No, that's alright." Betty Lou looked at me and shrugged.

After finishing lunch, I paid the bill, and we took off for the Palm Beach police station. Borman met us in the lobby.

"Hey, Drake, good to see you again. And Betty Lou, why I haven't seen you in ages." Borman shook my hand and gave Betty Lou a friendly smile. "So is working for the Marlow's like father like son?"

Betty Lou spied me out of the corner of her eye. "Not quite," she said.

"Well, come on into the office." Borman led us down the hall to his office, where we sat. "What can I do for you?"

"This time, Chief, I think there's something we can do for you." I pulled the photos from my pocket and handed the packet to Borman.

"What are these? Pictures of your vacation in the Catskills?" He chuckled as he opened the packet and withdrew the images.

"Hardly. What you have could be evidence in Stanley Carmichael's death."

"Oh?" Borman carefully examined each photo, then gazed intently at me. "Mind explaining what happened and why you took these photos?"

"Well, Chief, undressing to go for a swim, I noticed bruises on my shoulders. Then you told me about the rectangular marks on Stanley Carmichael's shoulders. I put two and two together but knew you'd need solid evidence. That's why I took the photos."

Borman sat back. "I'm missing something here. How'd *you* get the bruises?"

Betty Lou elbowed me. "Tell him about Bluto, Boss."

"Bluto?" Borman's eyes widened, and he leaned forward. "I definitely want to hear this."

"I don't know his real name, Chief. I just call him that. He's a large, muscular man who assaulted me in my pool last week. Let me explain."

Borman attentively listened while I gave him a detailed description of the incident.

"So, why didn't you report it?" he asked.

"If I reported everything that happened to me in the course of an investigation, I'd never get any work done, and neither would you. I figure things like this come with the territory. But now that Carmichael and I have similar bruise patterns, I wanted you to see mine and tell you how they occurred."

"Good work. Do you know who Bluto is? Does he work for Della?"

"I canvassed my contacts, but no one seems to know who he is. I figure he's from out of town," said Betty Lou.

"Drake, I need you to file a report of your assault and describe Bluto in as much detail as possible to my deputy. May I keep these photos?" Borman held up the packet.

"Of course, but I'll keep the negatives."

Borman withdrew the negatives, slipped them into an envelope, and handed them to me. He pressed a button on his intercom. "Deputy Miller, please have Sgt. Holcomb come to my office."

"Sir," said Holcomb as he entered.

"Please take Mr. Marlow's statement on his assault and start a file on his case. Include these photos and a note to cross-reference his case to that of Stanley Carmichael." Borman held out the photos.

Holcomb took them.

"Mr. Marlow, please follow me," said the Sgt.

"Don't worry about me, Boss. I'll simply sit here and catch up with an old friend." Betty Lou smiled as I rose.

Holcomb led me down the hall to his desk and put a form in his typewriter. He appeared to be the no-nonsense type with little chit-chat or desire to get to know me.

"What's your full name, address, and occupation?" he asked without looking at me.

Holcomb typed the answers to those and dozens of other questions onto the form. Surprisingly, he could give Betty Lou a run for her money on his words-per-minute typing speed. Forty minutes later, the unfriendly deputy had everything I could remember about my encounter with Bluto.

"Ready?" I asked Betty Lou upon returning to Borman's office.

"Sure thing. So nice to see you again, Chief." Betty Lou stood.

"Hopefully, it won't be this long between talks next time." Chief Borman rose and extended his hand to Betty Lou. His grasp lingered, and a brush of pink rose on her cheeks.

Unusually quiet, Betty Lou glided through the parking lot toward Celia.

"You like him," I said as we reached the car.

"He's nice. I haven't seen him in a long time, so we enjoyed catching up." Betty Lou kept a straight face as she slid into the passenger seat.

"Uh-huh. You know Borman's a widower." I engaged the engine.

"You don't say."

Neither of us spoke of Borman on our way back to the office. Once we arrived, Betty Lou exited the car while I remained seated.

"I think I'll drop by and see Constance. All those questions I wasn't able to ask her in the diner still need answers, and—"

"You want to see how she's feeling," said Betty Lou, finishing my sentence. "I understand."

"Strictly business."

"Trying to convince me or yourself?" She stood by the car, grinning.

I drove off without answering.

CHAPTER 19

Before leaving Palm Beach, I stopped at a pay phone, looked up Constance's address, and then drove back across the bridge into the city. I parked on Fern Street in front of the large two-story clapboard home with dormers and a wrap-around porch. The building appeared freshly painted light yellow with a sign on the front lawn that read: *Rose Crippen's Boarding House for Women*.

I strolled down the wide sidewalk, climbed the steps, and knocked on the screen door.

An elderly gray-haired woman, wiping her hands on a striped dish towel, came to the entry.

"Hello, I'm Mrs. Crippen. How can I help you?"

"I'm Drake Marlow. I'm here to see Constance Grimly if she's available." I held my hat and fingered the brim.

"You a co-worker or relative?" The woman gazed at me guardedly.

"Friend. I'm a friend. I heard she was ill and came to see how she's doing." I gave Mrs. Crippen my warmest smile.

"Wait here, and I'll see if she's receiving guests." The woman turned, supported herself with the railing as she climbed the stairs, and disappeared around a corner at the top landing. A few minutes later, she descended. "Constance will be right down. You can wait for her in the parlor." The screen door groaned as she opened it.

I followed her into the spacious parlor containing two seating areas, an upright piano, a table for playing cards, and a radio. A vase of summer flowers sat on the piano. Their light fragrance mingled with the odor of baking bread, permeating the room.

"Please have a seat. Constance should be down shortly. I have dinner in the oven, so you'll have to excuse me."

"Of course," I said, watching Mrs. Crippen wind her way toward the back of the parlor and out a door.

As I scanned the nicely furnished room, the house appeared clean and well-maintained. When I moved to Atlanta over ten years ago, I lived in a men's boarding house for a year before saving enough money to move into a one-bedroom apartment. I enjoyed the company of the others in the boarding house, and we had lots of good times, but it was sometimes noisy. While remembering those days, Constance walked in. A flower print dress fell lightly over her curvaceous body, drawn in at her narrow waist by a lime green belt. I stood, trying to calm my pounding heart.

"Mr. Marlow, to what do I owe your visit?" Constance's face flushed, but I couldn't tell if that was because of me or her cold. She walked to a side chair and stood next to it. "I don't want to get too close because of the cold. It's waning, but I want to be cautious." Due to the cold, her voice resonated with a deeper, sexier tone, which I liked.

"We went to the diner today hoping to speak with you about Della. Susan told us you weren't feeling well. How are you doing?"

"Better, thank you. Please sit down." This time, we both sat. "You said 'we' went to the diner today."

"Yes, Betty Lou and I. I believe you know my secretary."

"We've met."

"As you know, Della is my client, and I'm still working on her case. If you're up to it, I'd like to ask you a few more questions about your friendship with her."

Constance sniffed, took out a hanky, and wiped her reddened nose. "Sure."

"Could you tell me how you two met? What you talked about?" I placed my hat on the couch beside me and pulled out my notepad and fountain pen.

"I believe I mentioned that we were roommates. Someone must have introduced us. I don't remember who, but we were both looking for an apartment and decided to rent one together to save money." Constance massaged her hanky.

"So you didn't know each other before renting the apartment?"

"No. But it must have been divine intervention."

I nodded. "How'd you wind up here in the boarding house?"

"After Della moved out to marry Mr. Carmichael, I couldn't afford the rent alone, so I gave up the apartment and moved here. It's nice, quiet, and I can walk to work."

"You told me you and Della roomed together for about a year. I wondered what you did for entertainment. Did you ever go out together, say shopping or to the movies?"

Constance thought for a moment. "Della kept very much to herself in the beginning. Of course, she worked at the dance hall, so I guess that was her entertainment. She'd read, take a bus to the beach, or listen to the radio on her days off. Occasionally, we'd go to a movie. All that changed when she became chummy with the girls at the dance hall and started doing things with them. Then she met Mr. Carmichael. After that, she was out with him every spare moment until she married." Constance delivered her recollection with a trace of sadness.

"Who did the grocery shopping and cooking?" I asked.

"I did most of it in the beginning. We'd pool our money, and then I'd go to the market. I also did the cooking. Of course, when Della started seeing her lady friends, they'd go out together. Mr. Carmichael took up where the ladies left off."

"Did Della ever talk about where she grew up?"

Constance raised her eyes as though in thought. "I think she mentioned northern Florida once but didn't say much more about it except that she was glad to be away from there."

"What about her parents? Did she ever mention them?"

"Not that I recall," said Constance, shaking her head. "I got the impression they had passed."

"Do you know anything about her not liking hospitals or doctors?"

A spark of remembrance fluttered in her eyes. "You know, I do remember this one time. She hurt her leg dancing, so I urged her to see a physician. She wouldn't go, and there was something strange about how she reacted to my suggestion."

I sat forward. "What do you mean?"

Just as Constance was about to answer, an unexpected knock sounded at the front door.

"I'll get it," Constance called to Mrs. Crippen. "Please excuse me. I'll be right back."

She rose and went to the door. After some muffled conversation, Constance reentered the parlor carrying a small bouquet of red roses wrapped in white tissue paper. She sniffed at the blooms, but I doubted she could smell their fragrance with her cold. Behind her was a man who appeared at least five years younger than me. My heart sank as I stood. I'd never even considered the possibility that Constance had a beau, even though she was a lovely person inside and out.

She kept her eyes on the roses as she made introductions. "Mr. Wilcox, this is Mr. Marlow. He's a private investigator and came to ask me a few questions regarding one of his clients. Mr. Marlow, this is Mr. Wilcox. He's with the electric company."

Wilcox extended his hand. I did the same, though mine was more of a perfunctory gesture than one indicating 'happy to make your acquaintance.'

"Is there anything else, Mr. Marlow?" Constance lifted her gaze. Her soft aqua eyes seemed to apologize. Or was it my imagination?

"No. Thank you for your time, Miss Grimly. I hope you feel better soon. I'll see myself out."

~~~

"So, how'd it go with Constance?" Betty Lou peered across her desk with an expression of high expectation as I entered the office.

I slumped into a chair across from her desk. "Good and bad," I said.

"And that means?"
~~~

I looked up. I'm sure Betty Lou could see the despair in my eyes. "She's got a boyfriend."A loud gasp escaped Betty Lou as she clasped her hands to her mouth.

"Yep. He came to see how she was doing while I was questioning her about Della. He brought her roses."

"Oh, my." Betty Lou clucked her tongue and shook her head. "What did you do?"

"What could I do? I left."

Betty Lou rose, moved around her desk, and sat in the chair next to me. She squeezed my hand. "Just because he brought her flowers doesn't mean you're out of the picture or Constance doesn't want to see you. All this means is the man dropped by unexpectedly and brought her a lovely get-well gift. In a way, this was a good thing."

"A good thing? He brought her red roses. What did I bring her? Questions! How in the world could you conclude that was a good thing?" I gazed at her through narrowed eyes.

"Well, now that you know about the other man, and she knows you know, it will help you both decide what to do about each other. Kind of a clearing of the haze between you. You'll see that this was a good thing in the end." Betty Lou gave my hand a warm squeeze before returning to her desk.

"Humph."

"Now, what did you learn about Della?" Betty Lou placed her elbows on her desk and rested her chin in her cupped hands.

I sighed, withdrew my notepad from my jacket pocket, and flipped it open to my notes. I explained all I could about the questions I'd asked and the answers Constance gave me.

"It seems curious Della would have two such strong reactions to doctors and hospitals. Something traumatic must have happened," said Betty Lou.

"I agree, but the problem is we don't know what that trauma was, and it could hold the key to discovering who she is."

Betty Lou and I sat in silence, mulling over that thought. Suddenly, she lurched upright.

"Now that we know about the incidents, I might be able to use them when I question Della's lady friends. We'll get to the bottom of this, Boss. I promise you that!" Betty Lou gave me a staccato nod for emphasis.

~~~

That night, I drove to Willie's house in the Freshwater District of West Palm Beach, where upper-class Negro families lived. As I pulled to the curb, Celia's headlights bounced off the two-story brick structure with white trim fronted by a maintained lawn bordered by flowers and a low white picket fence. Willie's stock market investments had certainly paid off.

With no streetlights in the neighborhood or glow from Willie's porch light, the only illumination came from a half-moon as I made my way up the sidewalk toward the house. The front door creaked open when I reached the porch. In the doorway, Willie's silhouette greeted me, backlit by diffused light from a room down the hall.

"Come on in," he said, stepping back so I could enter. He peered left and right down the street, then quickly closed the door behind me.

With the shades pulled, the house was dark except for the muted light as Willie led me into a large kitchen with an eat-in dining table that sat six. Willie gestured for me to sit at one end.

"Want some coffee?" he asked.
~~~

"Nothing for me, thanks. Your family in bed?"

"Best they don't see you or hear our conversation."

Willie took a seat at the head of the table. "Now, what's this assignment you have for me?"

"I'm looking for someone," I said.

"Negro or white?"

"White."

Willie bristled at my answer. "I don't know how much help I can be. If he were a colored man, no problem, but a white man? We hardly run in the same circles."

"I understand. Chief Borman is also looking for him, but your network is much larger, and your communications much faster than his limited police force. Someone might have seen him, or at the least, your network could keep an eye out for him. He'd be hard to miss."

"Oh?"

I described Bluto in as much detail as possible.

"Well, even without his real name, with his size and scar, he sounds like someone who'd stand out." Willie chuckled. "So, why you lookin' for him?"

"We had a little run-in. I'd like to repay him."

Willie sat back and raised his hands, palms up. "You know we don't do that kind of work, Mr. Marlow."

"No, no, Willie. I don't want him roughed up. I want to repay him by having him arrested. All I need to know is where he is. That's all. Betty Lou tried to find him through her Palm Beach network and came up empty. She thinks he may be from out of town."

Willie folded his hands and placed them on the table. "I thought your interest was in Della Carmichael."

"It is. Bluto assaulted me because of her, then warned me to back off the investigation. I believe his threat has everything to do with why she hired me."

Willie was quiet.

"I need to tell you one more thing, Willie. Aside from my assault, this guy may have been involved in Stanley Carmichael's death."

The whites of Willie's eyes glowed large in the kitchen light. "Murder?"

"It's possible. I've gathered some evidence that indicates Bluto might be involved, but I don't have anything concrete. If Borman can arrest him for my assault, he may be able to squeeze the other information out of him."

Willie hesitated a moment, then leaned forward and spoke in a whisper. "As you know, my network operates in the shadows. We're very broad and very effective. We'll find Bluto if he's anywhere between the Palm Beaches and Key West, but you cain't question where I get my information."

"Never have, never will." I rose and followed Willie to the door, turning just before leaving. "Thank you," I said.

Willie nodded. "I'll let you know as soon as we've located him."

CHAPTER 20

Betty Lou and I sat in my office the following morning—me with my feet on the desk, ankles crossed, her in a side chair. We sipped coffee while I recounted my meeting with Willie.

"That's great, Boss. I'm sure he'll find Bluto, especially with the help of his next-door neighbor."

I looked quizzically at Betty Lou. "How do you know who lives next to Willie, and what does that have to do with him helping us?"

"Look, things changed a lot around here while you were away. Prohibition altered—well—just about everything in the country, including the Palm Beaches."

"You don't have to tell me," I said. "You do remember the bullet hole in Celia's door."

"I do. By the way, when are you going to get that fixed? Rain will ruin your upholstery if it gets inside."

I rolled my eyes. "Stick to the subject, please."

"Well, when you told me you were meeting Willie at his home, I looked up his address. The street seemed familiar, and then it came to me. I remembered a case your father took during the early days of Prohibition. His client lived on the same street. In fact, he lives just one door down from Willie. Guess who that is."

Betty Lou loved to play these guessing games. I didn't. "Who?" I asked, not really caring.

"Cracker Johnson."

My feet flew off the desk, and my chair became abruptly upright. I'd have soared onto the floor without the desk stopping me.

"Willie's next-door neighbor is *the* James J. 'Cracker' Johnson?"

"The one and only," said Betty Lou, giving me a 'you didn't know that, did you?' smirk.

The man had become a legend in West Palm Beach. Not only was he the most affluent Negro in the county, but his wealth surpassed most whites. He also wielded substantial power within both the colored and white communities.

"You do know why they call him 'Cracker' Johnson, don't you?" Betty Lou asked.

"White father, colored mother."

"And how did he make his money."

"He had a bar down on Second Street before Prohibition," I said.

"Humph. That's only a minuscule part of his empire. He owns property all over the state, purchased with proceeds from running bootleg whiskey into the county from the Bahamas. He also has a still somewhere in the glades that produces hundreds of gallons of hooch daily. He operates a pawn shop, runs an illegal bolita game, and makes loans."

I let out a whistle. I knew of his reputation but was flabbergasted at the man's amassed holdings.

"How in the world do you know so much about Cracker Johnson's businesses?"

"He was a client of your father's once at the beginning of Prohibition when the sheriff threatened him with arrest for selling illegal booze. Your father negotiated a settlement with the sheriff. Johnson got off, but he had to give up certain enterprises. He paid for your father's legal services with a case of British whiskey."

"You do know what you're telling me falls under attorney/client privilege," I reminded Betty Lou.

"I'm not an attorney, and your father is retired. Besides, what Cracker Johnson does for a living is pretty much common knowledge."

"If what you say is true and most of his activities are illegal, especially the Spanish gambling game bolita, why hasn't he been arrested?"

"And upset the tranquility of West Palm Beach? The sheriff would rather look the other way than arrest Cracker Johnson and have all of the Palm Beaches in an uproar. Why, who do you think supplies liquor to the Palm Beach Hotel, the Breakers, and the Everglades Club? Besides, the man does a lot of good for the community and is quite the philanthropist. He gives money to those in need and hands out scholarships to bright Negro students. He even loaned the county $50,000 once to balance the budget."

"I see. And you think this law-breaking philanthropist will help Willie find Bluto?"

"I wouldn't be surprised if he's the first person Willie turns to for help. Who do you think helped Cracker Johnson invest all his money?"

My eyebrows spiked. "That sly fox," I said.

I knew Willie had invested his money wisely in the stock market, and his reserves buffered him from the Depression, but I knew nothing about him advising Johnson.

Maybe I should ask him for investment advice. That is when I make enough to invest.

"Of course, what I told you is just between you and me." Betty Lou glared at me with a stern eye.

"Naturally."

"Back to Bluto. Those two know lots of people. If Bluto is out there, they'll find him." Betty Lou got up to leave. "Oh, I meant to tell you, I'll be out the rest of the day, so you're on phone duty."

"What are you up to?" I asked.

"My assignment." Betty Lou walked out the door. "Toodle-loo," she said, waving to me over her shoulder.

Sitting alone in the office for the rest of the day and answering the phone was strange. I made the best of the situation, though, including phoning Della. I needed to speak with her, but unfortunately, she was still out of town. Her Chinese maid wasn't sure when she'd be back.

Some good news did come out of the afternoon. I scheduled an appointment with a potential new client. Not exactly the kind of case I enjoyed—a cheating wife—but it was income and would keep me busy while Della's case moved slowly through our investigative channels. The husband of the adulteress planned to come in tomorrow morning to give me the details and a retainer.

Before I left for the day, Betty Lou called.

"How are things going?" I asked.

"Peachy," she said with enthusiasm. "I'll be out another day but should have something by Friday."

"So you'll be in the office then?"

"That's the plan."

"Great. We may have a new case. I'm meeting with the client tomorrow."

"How wonderful. Maybe we should trade places, and you be the secretary."

"Not on your life," I said, chuckling.

~~~

"Mr. Dunbar, I've been expecting you. Come in." I stood and moved from behind my desk to greet the man that just entered the office. "Please, have a seat."

Mr. Henry Dunbar was a slight man in stature whom I figured to be in his late fifties. He had a receding hairline, ears too large for his head, and a large mole on the side of his nose. The blemish twitched every time his nostril flared, which occurred frequently.

"It's my next-door neighbor," said Dunbar. A twitch followed his nose flare, and his long, thin fingers gripped the chair so hard his knuckles turned white.

"If you already know your wife is cheating on you with your neighbor, why do you need to hire me?"

"No. No. You've got it all wrong. An anonymous neighbor is the one who told me my wife was cheating." Twitch.

"I see." I took out a pad of paper and my pen to take notes. "Mr. Dunbar, let's start at the beginning. What's your wife's name?"

"Claire. Claire Rose Dunbar. She's fifty-two. We've been married for thirty years." Twitch.

A nose twitch punctuated each sentence. I struggled to keep my eyes on my notepad.

"What exactly did this anonymous neighbor tell you about your wife?" I asked.

"He says a car pulls into the driveway every morning after I leave for work, and someone enters the house. The person comes out about an hour later with a satisfied look. Here's the neighbor's note he left under the windshield wiper of my car." Dunbar handed me a folded piece of paper.
~~~

The note confirmed what Dunbar said, but because the author wrote in block letters, it was difficult to determine whether a man or woman had composed the message.

"If only I could get my hands on that guy!" Dunbar jammed his right fist into his left hand, resulting in a resounding slap.

I jumped.

"Mr. Dunbar, please don't take things into your own hands. Have you asked your wife about this?"

"I can't bring myself to do that. You see, Claire doesn't act as if anything is different. The house stays clean, the laundry gets done, and she serves dinner on time. If something were going on, there would be signs, wouldn't there? Some little clue? There's nothing. Everything seems the same—her routine, her demeanor. I need you to watch the house so I can confront her with hard evidence." Dunbar pounded his fist on the chair arm.

"Let me look into this for you, Mr. Dunbar, and see what turns up. First, though, I'll need a little more information."

"Of course."

After another thirty minutes of writing down the information I'd need to proceed with the investigation, I accepted a retainer from Mr. Dunbar and a photo of his wife and bid him adieu. I figured the stakeout job wouldn't take me long, maybe a couple of hours each morning for several days to establish a pattern of infidelity. The rest of each day would be devoted to Della's case.

Since lunchtime was close, I decided to go home and grab a sandwich. While there, I'd check my film supply and load the camera since I'd monitor the Dunbar's house first thing tomorrow morning.

CHAPTER 21

Stakeouts were the worst and best part of a private investigator's job. The worst was because you're primarily bored, waiting for something to happen, which could take hours, days, or weeks. Then, when the action started, your adrenalin pumps, and you can finally do your job. That's the best part. While I didn't look forward to this stakeout because of the reason—a cheating spouse—I knew I'd discover the truth. And, after all, that's what I was getting paid to do.

I parked Celia between several cars down the street from Mr. Dunbar's home, hoping my chariot wouldn't stand out. My pad, pen, binoculars, and camera, fitted with new film, sat on the seat next to me, ready at any moment. When Mr. Dunbar left the house, I noted the time and discretely snapped several photos of him pulling out. While cameras were helpful, I mainly relied on my observation, attention to detail, and notes.

After Mr. Dunbar left for work, I sat for another forty-five minutes before a gray Model A Ford pulled into the Dunbars' driveway. Steadying my binoculars, I waited for the man to get out.

Instead, a lady opened the door, went to the car's trunk, withdrew a cardboard box, and proceeded down the sidewalk to the front door. Besides her just over five foot height, slight build, and attire—a print dress and flats—I couldn't tell much about her as the box obscured her face. She walked to the house and entered without knocking. An hour later, the woman left, again with the package. I took a few photos, then returned to the office.

I spent the rest of the afternoon calling local establishments to learn more about Della. I came up empty. Hopefully, when Betty Lou returned tomorrow, she'd have discovered something to go on.

The following morning I planted myself in front of the Dunbar house again. The same woman arrived and exited the house within the timeframe she did the day before. I took photos of her and noted her arrival, departure, and appearance—this time, wearing a hat.

When I returned to the office, Betty Lou was at her desk. "I've been waiting for you," she said.

"Want to tell me about your time with the ladies?" I asked.

"Do I!" She scurried around her desk and followed me, carrying a notepad and pen. "By the way, where have you been?"

"Remember the client I told you about? Well, I've been on a stakeout." I placed the binoculars, camera, and notepad on my desk.

"What kind of case?"

"Infidelity," I said, sitting.

"Too bad." Betty Lou's lips drooped into a frown as she sat. "Discover who it was?"

"Not really. The neighbor who wrote Mr. Dunbar a note told him his wife was having an affair, but it turned out to be a lady coming to the house. It looked like she and Mrs. Dunbar were meeting. I'm going to stakeout the house for a few more days. If the lady turns up again, I'll let Mr. Dunbar know he has nothing to worry about, but he should talk to his wife so she can name the mysterious visitor." I lit a cigarette and blew a cloud of smoke into the room.

"My turn," said Betty Lou, flipping pages of her notebook.

I sat forward. "I'm all ears."

Betty Lou cleared her throat. "As it turns out, Della and her lady friends play bridge together on Wednesday and Thursday afternoons. Since Della was out of town, they needed a fourth. Guess whose name came up as a substitute?"

Just what I needed. Another one of her guessing games.

"Whose?" I asked, playing along.

"Why, mine, of course!" Betty Lou's eyes sparkled as she jutted her chin and gave me a Cheshire cat grin.

"How'd you manage that?" I asked, sitting back in amazement. To have wangled a seat at the bridge table with these women was pure genius and something I'd have never been able to do.

"Trade secret, Boss, besides it's not important how I did it. What's important is what I learned."

While I was eager to know Betty Lou's 'trade secret,' I knew I'd have to wait for a more opportune time to acquire that information—like when she wanted something from me. Then I'd suggest an even trade.

"Fine. What did you find out?"

Betty Lou pulled her chair closer to the desk and spoke in a lowered voice as though what she was about to say was top secret.

"Well, we started with friendly chitchat. How long have you lived in Palm Beach, and where are you from? That sort of thing."

"You didn't tell them you worked for me, did you?"

"Boss, give me some credit. I told them I worked for an attorney until he retired. I didn't lie, but I didn't tell them everything either. Then I told them how much I appreciated being included in their bridge game since their friend was away. I asked them what kind of player she was, getting a little more personal with each question. All this while playing. These ladies are accomplished bridge players, and I had to be on my toes to match them. Fortunately, I play some pretty fine bridge myself, so I seemed to fit in, even scoring a grand slam!"

While I didn't play bridge—gin was my game—I knew what that was from watching my parents play with friends every Saturday night. A player declares she can win all the tricks—thus an uncommon accomplishment. I was impressed, but I needed some hard facts about Della.

"So you were able to get in tight with the ladies?"

"They're very nice and treated me like a friend instead of a stranger."

I tapped my fingers on the desk. "I'm more interested in what they said about Della."

"Not by direct information, mind you, but by inference, here's what I found out. Della came from a small town in northern Florida where she lived with an aunt but didn't say the town or the aunt's name. They did say something about pecan trees, if that helps."

"Pecan trees?"

"Yep. I wrote it right here," said Betty Lou, pointing at her notes. "And they said they met Della at the dance hall and became fast friends. They confirmed she used the name Warren at the dance hall, but Smith when not working to separate her personal and professional lives."

I nodded. "Seems logical. I'm sure many women employed at the dance hall did the same. Did you find out if she was a widow while employed at the dance hall?"

"Sorry, I didn't. But the four friends went window shopping on Worth Avenue the day Stanley died."

"Chief Borman already told us that. What I need to know is whether Della left at any time while they were there?"

"I couldn't find that out, at least, not yet. But the ladies did confirm she hated hospitals. They said Della was relieved that Stanley had died instead of being injured. That way, he wouldn't have had to spend days in the hospital. If he had, she wouldn't have been able to visit him."

I sat back. "Hmm. There's something peculiar about Della's aversion to doctors and hospitals. What else did you find out?"

"That's all," said Betty Lou, sitting back and closing her notepad.

"What do you mean, 'That's all?'"

"I mean, that's all. I didn't want to push too hard because I didn't want to scare them off. Besides, I enjoyed playing bridge with them."

"Yeah, on my dime." I crossed my arms over my chest.

"Well, technically, it's Della's dime." Betty Lou cocked her head to the side.

"Splitting hairs," I said.

"The good news is Della won't be back for another week, so they asked me to substitute for her again. I told them, yes."

I came to an abrupt upright position; my brows spiked. "So, you won't be in the office Wednesday or Thursday afternoons next week?"

"Boss, investigations like this take time. You know that. Besides, I'm winning their confidence. I'll be able to find out more next time."

I knew inquiries like this took time, and since I was committed to discovering who Della was, Betty Lou's repeated round with the ladies wouldn't hurt. Would it?

"I guess that's okay, but make it the last time." I gave Betty Lou a stern stare. "And please type up your notes and put them in the file."

"Sure thing." She rose and walked to her office.

Betty Lou's typewriter clicked away as I sat at my desk and wrote up my notes from the two days I'd staked out the Dunbar home. Of course, I'd show up again on Monday and Tuesday, but if nothing changed, I'd inform Mr. Dunbar of what I discovered and close the case. Seemed apparent to me that the neighbor was mistaken.

CHAPTER 22

Early Monday morning, I went to the Dunbar home with my thermos of coffee, a dry piece of toast, and my usual assortment of accessories—binoculars, camera, notepad, and pen. As before, I parked between cars across the street and watched discretely through the open window. Within minutes, Mr. Dunbar pulled out of his driveway. I noted the time. The familiar gray Model A Ford drove into the driveway an hour later, and the same woman got out. This time, she wore a dark blue cloche hat she pulled low, obscuring her eyes and facial features. I snapped a photo of her arrival, waited for her to leave, then took another picture. The same scenario followed on Tuesday. This time because of a morning shower, the woman carried an open umbrella, again obscuring her face.

I dropped the roll of film off at Mr. Stills's studio for development, then returned to the office and phoned Mr. Dunbar. Though I wouldn't have the photos for another few days, he deserved an update on my progress. I made an appointment with him to come to the office after work on

Friday when I'd have the photos, and we could discuss his case in more detail.

In the meantime, I phoned my former family physician, Dr. Homer. I hadn't seen him since I returned and wanted to re-establish him as my family doctor. Plus, I wanted to ask him some questions regarding Della's case. Fortunately, I was able to see him in the late afternoon.

~~~

"Drake, my boy, so glad to see you. I heard you were back in town." Dr. Homer, a lean man in his sixties wearing his white doctor's coat, greeted me in the reception room. His last patient had just left, and his receptionist was closing the office. His warm smile and sparkling green eyes were as welcoming as I remembered. "Come on back to the office."

He led me down a hallway with several exam rooms on either side, then to a small compact office with a desk, two chairs, and bookcases crammed with medical books.

"Doesn't look as though anything's changed," I said, scanning the room I was familiar with from childhood.

"Maybe not the look of the office, but things have changed dramatically since the Depression. Half of my patients don't even come in anymore, thinking they can wait out their illness since they don't have the money to pay for treatment. But that only leads to them getting worse, especially the children. I've tried to convince them to come anyway and that I'll make provisions for payment, but most don't want to be beholding."

"It seems the Depression has taken its toll on everyone except those living in Palm Beach." For that, I was grateful, given my line of work.

"But there is some positive news," said Dr. Homer. "Last year was the first clinical trial of a new medicine called penicillin. It has great promise in treating harmful
~~~

bacterial infections. If it pans out, we'll have something that will save thousands of lives worldwide."

"Sounds exciting," I said, though I was more interested in obtaining information to help Della's case.

"It is, my boy, but you didn't come to talk about medicines. Before your parents left for Europe, they told me you opened a private investigation firm, and when you called, you said something about a case you're working on. How can I help?" Dr. Homer's bespeckled eyes crinkled at the corners as he smiled.

"I'm not sure. All I've got so far are bits and pieces, but I figured you'd at least be able to point me in the right direction."

"I'll do my best."

"I'm working with a woman who doesn't know who she is. I haven't been able to unearth her background, except that she may have come from northern Florida. She also has an aversion to physicians and hospitals, as though some trauma happened there. Do you have access to a list of doctors and hospitals in northern Florida? Whatever happened to her was probably in a town close to pecan trees. I'm thinking somewhere between the Atlantic coast and the panhandle."

"I'd suggest you bring her in so that I can evaluate her, but it sounds like she wouldn't come."

"I doubt she'd get anywhere close to a physician's office. Besides, she's not in town right now. If I had a list of physicians in the northern part of the state, I could call them and see if they'd had her as a patient."

Dr. Homer rubbed his jaw. "As a Florida Medical Association member, I have a directory of Florida doctors I can let you borrow. And perhaps you can contact the organization to see if they have a list of hospitals."

"I'd be most grateful. I need to find out what happened up there so she can get the help she needs."

"Your client is fortunate to have an investigator like you who cares for her beyond the money she's paying."

I wasn't sure that was me, but I accepted the compliment. "Thanks, and it was good to catch up with you, doctor."

"You also said you wanted to re-establish yourself here as a patient. Everyone needs an annual physical to ensure all is well. You should schedule one. You don't want to be caught behind the eight ball, even though you appear to be a healthy young whippersnapper." Dr. Homer chuckled as he put his stethoscope away.

"Thanks for the suggestion. I'm too busy to make an appointment now, but I'll call your receptionist as soon as I finish this case." I extended my hand; we shook.

"Wait here, and I'll get that directory for you." Dr. Homer walked out the door, returned moments later, and handed me the booklet. "I hope this helps."

"Can't thank you enough, Dr. I'll get this back to you as soon as Betty Lou and I finish with it."

I slipped into Celia on a high note, knowing I now possessed information that could potentially break Della's case.

That night after eating dinner, I spread out a Florida map on my dining table accompanied by the physician's directory. I circled the towns with physicians that fell within the corridor of northern Florida from the east coast to the panhandle. Next, I jotted down the doctor's name, phone number, and address. I noted physicians in cities and towns like Jacksonville, Lake City, and Live Oak toward the Atlantic; Tallahassee, Quincy, and Chattahoochee, in the middle; Defuniak Springs, Crestview, and Milton in the panhandle. I had no idea where I'd find the pecan trees, but pursuing that issue would have to wait until tomorrow. Right now, my hands were full, copying down all this information.

~~~

"Good Morning, Boss." Betty Lou walked to her file cabinet like she did every morning and placed her lunch and handbag into the drawer. "I hope you had a nice weekend."

"A busy weekend." I waggled my pages of notes in front of her, then dropped them onto her desk.

"What's that?" she asked, sitting. She moved her reading glasses from the top of her head to her nose, picked up the pages, and thumbed through them.

"While you were having dinner with Chief Borman, I was working."

She gazed at me through slitted eyes. "How'd you know about that?"

"Word travels fast in a small town."

"That Cookie! There are no secrets between you two." Betty Lou clucked her tongue.

I pointed to the list. "That's what will keep us busy for the next week. Those pages contain the names of physicians in the northern part of the state. One of them must have treated Della. The only thing missing is I don't know which towns are close to any pecan orchards."

"Why didn't you say so, Boss? I know how to find that out." Betty Lou reached into a desk drawer, pulled out a long green metal file box, and placed it on her desk.

"Where you'd get that?" I asked, pointing at the receptacle I'd never seen before.

"Brought it with me from your father's office."

"What's in it?"

"A treasure trove of information—names, addresses, and phone numbers of your father's prior clients, witnesses, experts, and anyone he dealt with in the legal or law
~~~

enforcement profession." Betty Lou pulled open the drawer and fingered through dozens of cards. "Ah, here he is—Dr. Pecan." She withdrew one of the cards and handed it to me—

Carl Middleton, Ph.D.; Professor/Dean, College of Agriculture; University of Florida

Specialty –Pecan Trees

"How in the world?" I'm sure Betty Lou noticed my surprised look.

"The professor was an expert witness in a case your father tried a dozen years ago." She pulled a phone directory from her desk, flipped open the pages, and motioned for me to return the card. She fingered down the page, wrote something on the card, and handed it back to me. "Now it's updated," she said.

The card read: *Retired to Palm Beach 1925; President, Palm Beach Garden Club.* Included was the professor's address and phone number.

Too stunned to speak, I carried the card to my office, pondering the goldmine Betty Lou's file box contained. If anyone knew the name of a town near a pecan orchard in northern Florida, Professor Middleton would.

While Betty Lou typed up my notes, I phoned the Florida Medical Association. They relayed the towns in the northern corridor that had hospitals. I also called Professor Middleton. He invited me to his home, saying we could talk more there about the nuts. I got the impression he missed teaching and wanted to recreate his classroom—even if it was with only one student. But then, I had a few hours to kill. During my visit, I hoped he'd be able to supply enough information to steer me in the right direction.

~~~

"Come in, lad," he said, opening the door. The dean's twinkling blue eyes behind dark-rimmed glasses
~~~

belied his age, which I guessed was in the mid-seventies. The spry professor was a wiry man with wisps of brown hair combed over a balding head. A red bow tie and a multi-colored sweater vest accented his khaki pants and white shirt, reminding me of the proverbial professor standing behind a classroom podium.

"Did you know that there are dozens of varieties of pecans? Or that it's the only naturally growing major tree nut in North America?"

"I didn't," I said as I entered the professor's bungalow-style home, where I anticipated learning a great deal of fascinating information about the pecan during my visit.

"Well, follow me, and we'll talk all about pecans," he said, beckoning me with his index finger.

I followed him through the house, out the back door, and into a building in the backyard that appeared more like a large shed with windows. Tucked under one window, a desk with its surface covered in books, paperwork, and a phone, took up space on one side of the room, while a work table ran the width of the building at the opposite end. Between them, shelves of books with diverse agricultural volumes, including some on pecans, lined the walls.

"This must be your laboratory," I said with a chuckle.

"Not far from it. Please have a seat." He pulled a folding wooden chair from a space between his desk and bookshelves and opened it.

I sat.

"Well, this seems a great place to work. Private and quiet."

"It's where I do most of my research and planning. Out back there"—the professor pointed out the window to rows of large containers holding plants—"is my real laboratory."

"Are those pecan trees?"

"Yep. Henry Elliott, a lumberman from Milton, Florida, cultivated the first pecan tree in Florida in 1912. The Elliott pecan is the most disease-resistant variety of pecan tree available. Farmers planted orchards with this variety all along State Highway 1 and even into Georgia. I'm creating a new pecan tree by grafting another hearty variety onto the Elliott pecan. Of course, we won't see the results for ten to twelve years."

"I had no idea a pecan tree took so long to produce nuts."

"When the trees are big enough, I'll take them to my farm in northern Florida, where I have a pecan orchard. That's where my son lives. He'll plant them and gather the fruit when they're mature. I probably won't see the first nut, but pecan trees can live hundreds of years, so my children, grandchildren, and great-grandchildren will enjoy them. How about an Elliott pecan?" The professor handed me a glass bowl of shelled nuts.

I took several and popped them into my mouth. He did the same.

"Delicious," I said.

"The Elliott pecan is one of the best, and they're a great source of nutrients, minerals, and vitamins that sustain health." The professor then explained the different types of pecans—their size and type of shells, and how the pecan is cultivated, harvested, shelled, and packaged for consumption.

I enjoyed eating pecans raw or in cookies and pastries, but I never thought about where they came from or how they made it to the table. The professor's animated delivery made it all the more fascinating.

"You've just had Pecan Cultivation 101," he said. "You were a good student. Now, how can I help you, young man?" The professor gazed at me intently.

I explained what I wanted to the professor and wondered if he could identify several northern communities near a pecan orchard.

"I can pinpoint the towns where you might want to concentrate your search."

"That would be terrific." I spread out my map of Florida on the professor's work table. "The circled towns indicate a physician or hospital in the town."

The professor leaned over and circled the town of Milton. Interestingly, I had also encircled the panhandle town as it had a physician. He then circled several other towns east of Milton, but intuition told me Milton was where I needed to start.

"If you ever get up that way, let me know, and you can visit the farm. My son, Ron, would happily put you up and show you around."

"That's very generous, professor. I may head up that way as part of my investigation. If I do, I'll let you know." I folded my map.

"I'll be curious to know how you make out," said the professor, handing me a small bag of pecans.

"Will do, and thanks. You've been a great help."

I nibbled on pecans and smiled as I drove back to the office. Between Dr. Homer and Professor Middleton, I'd had tremendous success with Della's case in the last two days, and while there was much more to do, I knew we were on the right track. Tomorrow, I'd spend the day on the phone trying to identify the hospital or physician that treated Della. While Betty Lou spent her last afternoons playing bridge with Della's lady friends, I'd pick up the photographs of the Dunbar case from Mr. Stills. By Friday, we'd have much more to go on in Della’s case, and I’d meet with Mr. Dunbar and close his investigation.

CHAPTER 23

Wednesday proved very productive. I started my morning using Betty Lou's typed lists to make phone calls. Beginning in Milton, I worked my way east along the State Road 1 corridor, where my circles, indicating physicians, intersected with the professor's circles, representing pecan trees. So far, none of the physicians I'd spoken with had Della Warren, Smith, or Brown as a patient, but I was waiting for several to return my phone call, including the one in Milton. While the results weren't positive, they weren't negative either. In investigations, getting a 'no' was as important as getting a 'yes.' That meant I could mark those contacts off my list and move on. That's what I did.

During a mid-morning break, I received an unexpected call from Mr. Dunbar.

"I got another note," he said in an edgy tone. "I thought you said there wasn't anything to worry about."

"Same handwriting?"

"As far as I can tell."

"What did this one say

"Same thing—'Your wife is having an affair.'"

"Mr. Dunbar, I didn't see anything unusual. Let me stake out the house again tomorrow morning. Meet me at our arranged time at the office Friday evening, and I'll share everything I have."

"I'd better be getting my money's worth, Marlow."

"Sir, I've done everything we discussed. Meet me Friday, and if you're not satisfied with my explanation, I'll refund your retainer."

"Fair enough," said Dunbar before hanging up.

I was baffled. Had I missed something? While the Dunbar situation rolled around my mind, I hopped back on the phone and continued phoning North Florida physicians. Then, a realization struck me like lightning, forcing a palm smack to my forehead. How could I be so stupid? None of my last names for Della—Warren, Smith, Brown, or Carmichael—were her maiden name. I didn't even know what that was! How could I track her down without knowing that? I bowed my head and shook it in disgrace. A seasoned investigator would have realized that before he spent four hours making long-distance calls that cost a bundle.

"*UGH*!" I shook my fists in the air in frustration.

Pushing back my chair so hard it hit the wall, I stormed out of the office, grabbing my jacket and hat and slamming the door behind me. I sat behind Celia's wheel, stared out the windshield, and took several deep breaths. I needed to calm down. The fact that I had overlooked such a crucial point was nobody's fault but mine. That revelation coming on the heels of the second Dunbar note, made me question what kind of an investigator I was.

Starting up Celia, I drove over the bridge into West Palm Beach to Stills photography studio to pick up the pictures taken at the Dunbar home. Standing at the empty counter in the studio, I noticed a red light next to a door and a sign dangling from a hook—"IN DARKROOM. PRESS BUTTON FOR SERVICE."

I pressed the buzzer on the counter and heard Stills' muffled voice, "Be right there." He entered the studio moments later, wiping his hands on his apron. "Drake, good to see you. Your photos are all ready." He reached into a drawer behind the counter, pulled out a packet, and handed the envelope to me.

"Thanks," I said, exchanging the photos for payment.

"I saw something interesting in several of the photos and blew them up. You might want to pay special attention to those. No charge for the extra work."

"What did you see?" I asked, opening the packet.

Unexpectedly, the studio's front door opened, and a well-dressed couple entered. Stills looked at his watch.

"So sorry, Drake, but I'll have to call you later. Mr. and Mrs. Arlington have an appointment for their portraits."

Nodding to Stills and the Arlingtons, I bid them "good afternoon" and walked out of the studio. Back in the car, I withdrew the photos and scanned them. As expected, they were of Mr. Dunbar going to work and the mystery woman arriving and leaving the Dunbar home on consecutive days. They didn't seem to depict anything out of the ordinary. The images Mr. Stills enlarged showed a closeup of the mystery woman's left hand as she exited the home. Why had he honed in on that part of her anatomy?

Examining the photos more closely, I finally saw what Stills must have seen. On the first day of the stakeout, when the mystery woman left the Dunbar home, she didn't have a wedding band on her left hand. In the photo taken the next day, she did. Had she gotten married overnight?

I examined the pictures from the third and fourth days with the same results. One day the mystery woman wasn't wearing a wedding ring; the next day, she was. What was going on? I needed to return to the office, spread the photos on my desk, and look at them more carefully—this time, with the aid of a magnifying glass.

As I steered Celia from the curb, I realized I was only a few blocks from Woolworths, and it had been over a week since I'd visited Constance. Was she feeling better? Was she over her cold?

I turned down Clematis; Woolworths was dead ahead. As I got closer to the diner, a little voice in my head chastised me—"If you cared about Constance, wouldn't you have phoned or stopped by the diner or boarding house days ago and inquired about her well-being and not waited until a week or more had passed?"

"Yeah," I silently answered, *"but I've been busy"*—a truthful statement—*"and she already has someone who genuinely cares about her—red roses don't lie"*—another honest observation. Yet, I'd never shied away from a challenge or difficult situation as a kid or an adult. But that old voice got in the last word and reminded me of what tied me in emotional knots—*"You don't want to feel that gut-wrenching, rip-your-heart-out pain again caused by another woman, do you?"*

I drove past the diner.

Add one more item to the growing list of professional and personal failures.

When I arrived back at the office, I fanned out the photos on my desk, including the enlargements, according to the date I took them. Then I retrieved my magnifying glass. Hovering over the images, I inspected each slowly, deliberately. No detail escaped my attention. After the scrutiny, I plopped into my chair as though exhausted from the effort. My reaction, though, was more amazement and tied to the realization that I'd figured out what was going on—something completely unexpected. Yet, I couldn't prove my theory until I conducted a final stakeout tomorrow.

I gathered the photos, slipped them into the packet, and placed them in the desk's center drawer. Tomorrow, Mr. Dunbar would learn the truth about his wife's infidelity.

With nothing more to do on the Dunbar case until tomorrow, I'd return home and go for a swim to clear my head. Later, I'd stop by the Green Turtle, have a light dinner, and see Cookie. Betty Lou would be back tomorrow with what I hoped would be new information that would help us pinpoint Della's past.

~~~

For a Thursday night in the middle of the Depression, the Green Turtle was surprisingly lively. The Depression had taken its toll on the country's economy. Yet, somehow Florida seemed to have been spared the worst of it. Being a state dependent on agriculture rather than industry seemed to make a difference, plus Florida had experienced a depression several years before the big one hit.

With the Florida banks failing during the land bust in 1926, three years before the nationwide Depression, residents had become all too familiar with making adjustments. The 1928 hurricane that took the lives of almost 3,500 residents around Lake Okeechobee in western Palm Beach County also prepared us for future hardships, resulting in a less dramatic impact. Thankfully, wealthy snowbirds from the Midwest and Northeast still owned property and came to Florida's southeast coast to keep Cookie, me, and others stay in business.
~~~

I grabbed a seat at the bar while most guests sat in the main dining room. A male pianist played a selection of background music—"How Deep is the Ocean," "April in Paris," and "Goodnight My Love"—as we dined.

"How's it goin', mate?" asked Cookie. He slipped onto a stool next to me.

"If you don't count the gross faux pas I've made today, not bad." I forked the last bite of my dessert into my mouth—Cookie's flaky crust seagrape tart.

"I've had a few of those in my time." Cookie rolled his eyes, but his understanding smile made me feel I wasn't the only one to do dumb things. "Say," he said, his blue eyes twinkling in the ambient light, "we've both been workin' hard lately and haven't been on an outin' in ages. Since we'll be closin' the restaurant for the month of August, just a few days from now, how 'bout we take a road trip?"

Cookie and I had always enjoyed our time together, but with Della's case hanging over my head, I wasn't sure I could afford the time away. On the other hand, if I heard from one of the physicians I'd contacted that Della had been a patient and Betty Lou returned with some revealing news, maybe a road trip to northern Florida would be in order.

"Perhaps," I said. "Give me a few days to wrap up a case I'm working on and see what return phone calls I get. You may just have a companion for your road trip."

"Wonderful, mate. I'll wait to hear from you." Cookie stood, patted me on the back, and returned to the kitchen.

I left the Green Turtle with a half smile. A whole smile would have to wait until I received the anticipated good news tomorrow.

CHAPTER 24

Early Monday morning, I gathered my stakeout gear—a thermos of coffee, snacks, binoculars, camera—and headed for the Dunbars. Parking in my usual location, I observed Mr. Dunbar leave the house and the mystery woman arrive. This time, a newspaper obscured a complete view of her face as she read today's news and walked down the sidewalk toward the house.

I waited.

Sure enough, just shy of an hour later, she left. After she pulled out of the driveway, I carried the Dunbar file with the photos to the house and knocked on the front door, ready to confront Mrs. Dunbar with the evidence. No one answered. I rapped again. Still no answer.

Peering through the front window and not noticing any movement, I walked down the driveway toward the rear of the house. Wearing a print dress covered by an apron, Mrs. Dunbar hung laundry on the backyard clothesline.

"Mrs. Dunbar?"

She wheeled around and gazed at me, her mouth and eyes wide open. "Who-o-o are you?" she stammered, clutching a wet towel.

"I'm Drake Marlow, a private investigator. Hey—wait a minute." I flipped open the file I held, pulled the photo of Mrs. Dunbar from it, and compared it to the woman before me. Same height. Same build. But the face was decidedly dissimilar. "You aren't Mrs. Dunbar. Who are you? And where's Mrs. Dunbar?"

"I'm Donna Stewart. I'm a friend of Claire's. She's—she's—" The woman's voice broke, and her eyes gazed toward the house.

"Don't even try to make a run for it." I peered at the woman with narrowed eyes and moved toward the back porch, positioning myself between her and the house. "I'll ask you again, ma'am. Where's Mrs. Dunbar?"

The woman hesitated. Her chin quivered, and then her whole body began to shake. She dropped the towel back into the basket, brought her hands to her face, and began to sob. "I knew this wouldn't work. I told Claire it was too risky and that someone would find out. But she insisted on doing it anyway. Now she's been caught." The woman gathered her apron and wept into it.

"Yes, she's been caught, and I'm obligated to tell her husband about this."

"Please, please don't tell him. It will significantly damage his self-esteem and ruin his and Claire's marriage." Her eyes pleaded with me as tears ran in rivulets down her flushed cheeks.

"Claire should have thought about that before launching this little charade." Knowing his wife had deceived him, I couldn't imagine how hurt Mr. Dunbar would be.

"Claire gave the circumstances a lot of thought," the woman countered between sobs. "But she simply had to do it."

"How did she get out of the house without someone seeing her? I've been watching it for days. I saw you come and go, but Claire never left the house." I looked at the woman's left hand. No wedding ring. Then as though a light bulb switched on, I realized why Stills had enlarged photos of the ladies' hands. "You two switched places! You'd walk into the house, and she'd walk out wearing the same dress. And to be cautious, you obscured your faces with a box, a hat, an umbrella, and today a newspaper."

"Just in case someone was watching," the woman said as she dabbed at her tears.

"Clever. But the jig is up, and your tears aren't stopping me from telling Mr. Dunbar about Claire's affair. Who's the other man?"

"Affair? Another man? What are you talking about, Mr. Marlow? Claire isn't having an affair."

"If she isn't, Miss Stewart, why is she sneaking out of the house several days a week? And why are you covering for her?" I glared at her with steely eyes.

The woman wiped her tears and sighed, softening her countenance. "How about a cup of coffee while I explain."

~~~

When I returned to the office, Betty Lou was furiously typing away. She stopped when she saw me enter.

"Hi, Boss. Thanks for the note letting me know where you were. I hope you had a productive morning."

"I did, but the conclusion was the strangest thing I've ever encountered. The ingenuity of some women to conceal a secret is mind-boggling." I scratched my head.

"We are a clever lot," said Betty Lou. "So what did you uncover?"

"I'll tell you about it when Mr. Dunbar arrives around five o'clock."
~~~

"Mr. Dunbar? He's the man whose wife is cheating on him?"

"One could say that, but I'm sure he'll be relieved when I tell him why. So what did you find out? Della hiding things, too?" I sat in a chair in our makeshift reception room.

"Is she!" Betty Lou leaned forward and was about to reveal what she had learned when the phone rang. Her shoulder's drooped in disappointment as she gazed at me and picked up the phone. "Marlow Investigations—Mr. Marlow? Yes, he's here." Betty Lou covered the receiver with her hand. "It's for you. Long distance. A Miss Anne Getting from Dr. Orbach's office in Milton, Florida."

I jumped up and rushed into my office. Out of breath, I lifted the receiver and announced, "Drake Marlow," into the phone. I could hear a click as Betty Lou replaced her receiver.

"Mr. Marlow, this is Miss Anne Getting. I'm Dr. Orbach's assistant. I understand you've been asking about a woman named Della." Her voice was low, almost but not quite a whisper, and had a distinct northern Florida accent. I had to listen intently.

"That's right. I don't know Della's last name, but she may have gone by the name Smith, Brown, or Manning." Adrenaline surged through me in anticipation of finally getting some answers. I poised a pen over my notepad.

"I see. Well, we did have a patient named Della many years ago, but she didn't have any of those last names."

"Can you tell me her last name?"

"Wright, Della Wright. I don't know if it's the same person you're trying to help, but I always thought what happened to her was the worst kind of betrayal."

I gulped. “What happened to her?”

“She was committed to Chattahoochee—sorry, I mean the Florida State Hospital—by court order. We never saw her again.”

“Do you know why she was sent to the hospital?”

“Not specifically. Her grandfather filed the commitment papers, but I believe she was—” There was a prolonged silence. “I’ve got to go, Mr. Marlow. I’ve probably told you too much already.”

“Wait! Miss Getting?” But the phone clicked, then went dead. I furiously thumbed through my notes and found Dr. Orbach’s office number. I called the long-distance operator and placed the call.

“Dr. Orbach’s office, Miss Glass speaking.”

“Hello, Miss Glass. I’m Drake Marlow, a private investigator from Palm Beach, Florida. I’m returning a call from your office. May I speak to Dr. Orbach’s assistant, Anne Getting?”

“Anne Getting? I’m sorry, Mr. Marlow, but Dr. Orbach doesn’t have an assistant by that name.”

“Is there someone else there with that name?” I nervously tapped my pen on the notepad.

“No. Maybe you’re thinking of another physician. Are you sure the call came from Dr. Orbach’s office?”

“That’s what the caller said.”

“Well, unfortunately, we don’t have anyone by that name, so I don’t think we can help you. I’m sorry.”

“I am, too.” Flummoxed, I hung up the phone.

“You okay, Boss?” Betty Lou stood on the threshold between our offices.

“I’m not sure,” I said, raking my hands through my hair. “Anne Getting abruptly hung up in the middle of our conversation. When I returned the call, the receptionist said no one by that name works at Dr. Orbach’s office.”

"Did you ask the receptionist about Della?"

"I would have, except obviously, something's amiss there. Besides, Miss Getting already told me what I wanted to know. It's just that I hoped to ask her more questions."

"Well, what did she say?" Betty Lou walked into my office and sat.

"She said they had a Della Wright as a patient, but she had been committed to the Florida State Hospital."

"Chattahoochee? Why?"

"I was trying to find out when Miss Getting hung up. But at least I know a possible name to go by. And, if Della was committed, it makes sense that she'd dread going to doctors or hospitals. Chattahoochee is a feared word in Florida. I can't imagine what happens in that place."

As a child, I distinctly remember parents telling their children if they didn't behave, they'd be sent to Chattahoochee. Just mentioning the institution sent fear through the heart of every child.

"Boss, that's what I was going to tell you. During my bridge game with the girls, I missed an important play. My partner said, 'That was a crazy play, Betty Lou. You don't want to do that again. We'll think you're loony and commit you to Chattahoochee like Della was.'"

"Did you ask your partner what she meant?"

"Of course. But she realized she'd said too much by that time, and when I followed up, she said it was just an expression and didn't mean anything. From then on, they clammed up. Now that Anne Getting has said the same thing, there must be some truth to it."

Betty Lou and I gazed at each other. We both knew what this information meant—time for a road trip. But first, I needed to meet with Mr. Dunbar and give him the results of my investigation into his unfaithful wife.

~~~
~~~

"Thank you for coming, Mr. Dunbar. Please come in and have a seat. I realize this isn't a pleasant time for you."

"No, it isn't," he said, "but I'd rather know the truth than live with suspicions."

I'd forgotten about his nose mole that twitched. I swallowed a smirk as I closed the office door, moved to my desk, and sat. My notes and packet of photographs lay in front of me.

"First, let me explain what I did in your wife's case to gather the evidence and confront her." I gave Mr. Dunbar a copy of my notes and the photos as I conducted daily surveillance. I explained the enlarged images and how they led to my going to the house to confront Claire with the pictorial evidence, only to find her hanging the laundry on the clothesline in the backyard. "When she turned around, I realized the woman wasn't Claire at all. She identified herself as Donna Stewart."

"Donna? Why she's Claire's best friend! What was she doing hanging out our laundry?"

"Seems she's been helping Claire with this—how shall I put it?—rather delicate issue."

"I'll say it's a delicate issue. When a man's been married as long I have and trusts his wife, infidelity is the last thing he expects." Mr. Dunbar crossed his arms over his chest and huffed out a grunt.

"It's not what you think, Mr. Dunbar. Your wife isn't having an affair. She's doing something she believes will benefit you."

"Benefit me? I'm confused. The anonymous note said Claire was having an affair."

"Well, if you want to think working part-time to earn extra money as having an affair, then so be it."

Mr. Dunbar jolted forward. "Working! Claire can't have a job. We discussed that, and I forbade it!" He pointed his index finger in the air for emphasis.

"I see," I said, readjusting myself. "Well, that's what's been happening. Your wife realized these were hard times, so she found a part-time job as a cashier at a grocery store. She couldn't get there without a car, so she enlisted Miss Stewart's aid."

"But, the housework, grocery shopping, laundry. They were all done like she'd been home all day."

"Ah, I can see the confusion. Donna would drive to your house in the morning, and Claire would take the car to work. During the day, Donna would do the housework while Claire worked. She'd return around four o'clock after putting in a half day's work and before you got home."

"But the photos don't lie. Claire never left the house." Dunbar pointed at the photos scattered on my desk.

"That's the interesting part. Claire and Donna changed clothes, so it looked like the same person had arrived and left the house in case someone was looking. And, I guess someone was—your neighbor."

"Aside from the fact that my wife disobeyed me, why did the neighbor lead me to believe she was having an affair?"

"That, Mr. Dunbar, can only be explained by your anonymous neighbor, but perhaps he or she wanted you to look closely at what was happening. Stating that your wife was having an affair would get your attention. It worked."

Suddenly, Betty Lou stuck her head into the office. "Excuse me, Mr. Marlow, but Mrs. Dunbar and Miss Stewart are here."

"Show them in, and please bring a chair from your office." I stood. So did Mr. Dunbar, with furrowed brow and tightened eyes, indicating he wasn't thrilled about his wife showing up.

"Hello, Kerney," Claire said softly upon entering. Mrs. Stewart followed. Both held their heads slightly downward.

"Claire," said Mr. Dunbar in a scolding tone. "Are you here to apologize for this most unbecoming behavior?"

Mrs. Dunbar looked up and squared her shoulders. She took a deep breath. "No, Kerney. I assure you I am not here to apologize, and I would do it again if the situation arose." Her eyes were focused, and her lips drew a thin line across her mouth.

Mr. Dunbar gasped. "Why, Claire, you've never talked to me this way before." Stunned by his wife's boldness, Dunbar plopped into his chair, nose flaring, mole twitching.

Miss Stewart, Betty Lou, and I stood speechless, eyeing the couple.

"You see," said Mrs. Dunbar, "I did it for you."

"For me?" Mr. Dunbar slapped his hand against his chest.

"Don't you have a birthday coming up?"

Mr. Dunbar nodded.

"And haven't you always wanted to see where your family came from in Dunbar, Scotland?"

Another nod.

"I got a job to make extra money to help make that happen." Mrs. Dunbar handed her husband an envelope.

Mr. Dunbar gazed curiously at the envelope, then opened it. "Claire, there are several hundred dollars here!" He stared at his wife wide-eyed.

"Yes. I've been working for quite a while now. Donna was only trying to help me make your trip a reality by handling the house chores so you wouldn't be suspicious. I wanted to surprise you."

"That you have," said Mr. Dunbar, rising. He wrapped his arms around his wife and drew her close. "I'm so sorry I doubted you, Claire. Please accept my apology."

"Oh, Kerney. I'd never do anything to disrespect you. I only wanted to give you a special birthday gift. One you'd remember." Mrs. Dunbar began to cry. Her husband held her tight.

Miss Stewart and Betty Lou wiped tears from their eyes. So did I.

Mr. Dunbar released his wife, withdrew two twenty-dollar bills from his wallet, and handed them to me. "I think this should handle the extra hours you put in. I won't be needing your services anymore."

"Of course," I said. I gathered the photos and notes, placed them in a large envelope, and handed them to Mr. Dunbar. Perhaps one day, he and Claire would have a good laugh over them.

After Betty Lou and I saw the Dunbars and Miss Stewart to the door, we returned to my office and sat.

"Whew," I said, swiping the back of my hand over my brow. "Glad that case ended happily."

"Me, too. Will you head to the Green Turtle to let Cookie know you two can take that road trip to the panhandle now?"

"Yep. We'll probably leave on Sunday, so don't expect me in the office on Monday. I'll call you from the road and update you on our progress."

"I'll hold down the fort while you're gone." Betty Lou rose and went to her office to gather her belongings. Before leaving, she poked her head in the door and smiled. "Good work today. Oh, and I forgot to tell you, Constance called just as you and Mr. Dunbar were meeting. She said she had some important news for you."

My heart began to race. "That's all she said?"

"That and to call her back on Monday. Have a safe trip, Boss." Betty Lou blew me a kiss as she left the office.

With a cigarette in one hand, glass ripe with whiskey in the other, and feet perched on my desk, I remained in the office reflecting on today's events: the successful outcome of the Dunbar case and the surprise call from Constance. I wondered what important news she had to tell me, but phoning her would have to wait until sometime next week. I still faced the road trip to the panhandle with Cookie and could only pray Della's situation would have as happy an ending as the Dunbars. However, considering all the secrecy and mystery surrounding her, I wasn't sure that would happen.

CHAPTER 25

Over the weekend, Cookie and I planned our trip hunched over an official road map from the Florida State Road Department. Realizing the journey would take a minimum of two days to get to Milton, driving at least eight hours each day, we figured we'd change drivers every three to four hours to relieve each other of the monotony. Cookie planned on packing a container full of sandwiches and snacks for our first day, and I had made arrangements with Professor Middleton for us to stay with his son, Ron, at their pecan farm, which was halfway between Milton and De Funiak Springs.

Our excursion would be an investigative and business road trip rolled into one. While I pursued my investigation, Cookie would connect with Ron, who could supply the delicious meaty nut to the Green Turtle, and he'd suggest that the restaurant be designated as a distributor of Middleton pecans to other local eateries and markets. That and the fact that Cookie had a vested interest in the subject of our journey—Della—would make the trip abounding with possibilities.

I hadn't heard back from Chief Borman or Willie before leaving Palm Beach and figured they hadn't had any luck finding Bluto. Realistically, only a few days had passed, and I couldn't expect miracles. If either of them located the big guy, I knew they'd call the office to let me know. I'd check in with Betty Lou daily to get any updates.

Early Monday morning, Cookie and I headed north on State Highway 4, typically known as U.S. Route 1, a two-lane paved road that hugged the east coast through most of Florida. Small towns, with less than a thousand residents, dotted the landscape connected by long stretches of straight, flat roadway lined with Florida scrub. Just south of Titusville, we turned onto State Road 22 toward Orlando, where we stopped for lunch at a quaint gas station/diner, stretched our legs, and gassed up. I also phoned Betty Lou to let her know where we were.

Afterward, we hopped on State Highway 2 toward Ocala. Leaving hundreds of miles of Florida's flatlands behind, it was a relief to drive through rolling hills. Since we were traveling toward the end of summer and the sun wouldn't set until late, we had plenty of sunlight for the long drive, though the proverbial summer thunderstorm occasionally slowed us down.

Following a good night's sleep in a roadside hotel in Ocala, we ate breakfast and took State Highway 19 north along the west coast of Florida. The inland road mimicked the curve of the Gulf of Mexico as it directed us north. How I wished it followed as close to the coast as State Highway 4 had. Then we could have seen the Gulf of Mexico.

"Hey, Cookie, you ever been to the Gulf?"

Cookie jerked his head up as though he'd nodded off. "Can't say that I have, mate."

"What do say we drive over and dip our toes into the surf on our return trip—just to say we've been there?"

"Like we did in Calais, France, after the war?"

"Yeah," I said. "Now, that was a road trip. Remember how all the women threw their arms around our necks and kissed us in appreciation of our fighting? We couldn't understand what they said, but their actions spoke louder than words." I let out a chuckle, remembering.

"And then there were those picnics on the beach with your Danielle," said Cookie, eyeing me with a raised brow.

"And your Francine," I said, giving him a wink.

"Yeah, that was some time, mate. We need to go on road trips more often."

We fell silent, each lost in our own memories of days past.

Just outside Tallahassee, Florida's capital, we stopped for lunch. Though we were still several hours from the Middleton Pecan Orchard, my body tingled with excitement, realizing we were getting closer to Milton. Deep in my bones, I knew I'd find answers in that small town and couldn't wait to get there and make some inquiries.

Thinking back to Della's initial visit to the office reminded me of this case's fundamental question: "If you're not Mrs. Stanley Carmichael, then who are you?"

I desperately wanted to answer that question for her.

By mid-afternoon, we turned off the main road and traveled about a mile before seeing a sign for the Middleton Pecan Orchard. Pulling onto a gravel road that wound through rows of tall pecan trees, we came to a large two-story, white, wood-framed house. A sizeable barn stood down an access road.

Chickens scurried out of the way, and a large brown dog bounded from the front porch and began barking as we pulled to a stop. Cookie's face turned pale, and he rolled up his window.

"Ron said he'd look ferocious but is really very friendly," I said, trying to assuage Cookie's fright. Once the dog reached the car, he stood on his hind legs, put his paws on my door, and looked through the open window at me. His tongue hung from open jaws, revealing substantial teeth.

"Here, Jake," a man called as he stepped from the porch.

Jake dropped from the car and loped toward the voice.

"You must be Drake. I'm Ron," said the man, reaching his hand through the window. We shook.

"And this is Cookie," I said, leaning back so Ron could see him.

"Well, come on in. We're all ready for you. I'm sure you'd like to rest after your long day on the road." Ron opened the car door and helped us retrieve our bags. Jake sniffed Cookie and me, wagged his tail, and followed our every move onto the porch before curling up on the stoop to resume his sentry. We went inside.

Ron introduced us to his wife, Georganne, his son, Bill, who had just graduated from high school, and his daughter, Susan, who had one more year left, then showed us upstairs. Our sleeping accommodation was a comfortable guest room with twin beds.

"The family bathroom is just down the hall," said Ron, pointing in its direction. "Why don't you get settled and then come downstairs? We'll take a spin around the farm before supper."

"Sounds great," I said.

The clock read five o'clock when Cookie and I descended the stairs. Betty and Susan were making dinner while Bill sat at the kitchen table. He stood as we entered.

"All set?" he asked, gazing at us.

"Ready whenever you are, mate," said Cookie, in his Aussie accent.

Susan turned, gazed at Cookie with striking green eyes, and giggled.

"He's from Australia," I said. "They all speak funny there."

"I didn't mean to be rude. It's just that I've never met anyone from Australia." A blush of pink bloomed on Susan's neck.

"Not a problem, darlin'. I'll tell you all about it over dinner," said Cookie, thickening his accent.

"Dad said he'd meet us at the barn," said Bill. "Mom, we should be back in about an hour."

Bill drove us to the barn in their pickup truck. When we arrived, Cookie, Ron, and I moved to the truck bed while Bill steered down rows of newly planted seedlings and stately, old, leafless pecan trees loaded with ripening nuts. All the while, Ron gave us a history of the property and a lesson on growing pecans.

"Harvest season is September to November, so these nuts are just about ready. After harvesting, they'll cure and then go to processing. I'll take Cookie to the processing barn tomorrow while you go to Milton. That way, he can see the entire process, and we can talk business."

"Just have one question about the harvesting. How do you get the pecans off the trees? You don't simply wait for them to fall, do you?" I asked.

Ron laughed. "No, that would take too long. We shake the branches, then pick up the fallen nuts with a pecan picker. It's very labor intensive, but the result is delicious."

"With the Depression, it's got to be a difficult time marketing pecans," said Cookie.

"It's difficult for all of us farmers right now. We're all dealing with overproduction and underconsumption. Loans from the government are helping, but farmers instinctively know they'll endure many lean years. The thing is, farmers never give up. We work through the bad times, knowing better times are ahead."

I appreciated Ron's optimism. Living in Palm Beach, one could get complacent during the Depression upon seeing so many wealthy people with money to burn. But the reality was that many Florida vegetable, citrus, dairy, and cattle farmers had already lost their farms to foreclosure because of the Depression. Life was difficult for most Americans, and I felt fortunate to have clients. We all endured as best we could.

Our tour ended, and we returned to the house for a meal of chicken and dumplings topped off with peach pie. In the morning, I'd head for Milton. I couldn't wait to see what the day would bring and whether I'd find some answers or this trip would prove to be a wild goose chase. I prayed it was the former.

~~~

Satisfied with a hearty breakfast of eggs, bacon, biscuits, and gravy, I headed for Milton. The town was forty miles away, and the drive took about an hour and a half. I pulled into a gravel parking lot beside a wooden clapboard house on the edge of town. A shingle with Dr. Orbach written on it hung outside a small added-on office at one end of the building. The sign creaked as it swayed slightly in the morning breeze.

Inside, the waiting room was small, with four unoccupied wooden chairs. The receptionist sat at one end of the room; Miss Glass was printed on a wooden nameplate on her desk.
~~~

"Good morning, Miss Glass. I'm here to see Dr. Orbach." I didn't want to introduce myself in case she remembered my name from our previous phone call. Miss Glass looked at me curiously as I fingered my hat in my hands.

"You're not from around here, are you?" she asked in a familiar Florida drawl.

"No. I just drove up from Miami and am staying at the Middleton farm. Unfortunately, I've developed a severe ache in my side and don't want to drive another mile until I know what it is." I grimaced and held my hand against my lower abdomen.

"Well, we do have other patients with appointments who will be arriving any moment, but the doctor can see you in less than an hour if you don't mind waiting. Please have a seat and fill out these forms." Miss Glass handed me a pencil and a clipboard with several forms.

"I'll wait. Thank you," I said.

While filling out the paperwork, a man in overalls and a woman with two children left the office, and other locals arrived. We exchanged greetings as they moved from the reception area to the exam room. Between patients, I scanned the office. The room was pleasant and clean, with a hat rack, a table with newspapers, striped wallpaper with pink roses, and several framed oil paintings of floral arrangements and landscapes that looked like an amateur artist painted them.

I returned the forms to Miss Glass, who took them into the back, then it was my turn.

Dr. Orbach, a middle-aged bespeckled man, opened the door to the reception area and called the fictitious name I'd put on the forms. He dressed in street clothes and wore an unbuttoned doctor's jacket frayed at the cuffs and not as white as one would expect. A stethoscope hung around his neck. As I followed him into an exam room, a lump formed in my throat, a mixture of excitement and trepidation at what I would discover.

Dr. Orbach scanned my paperwork, then looked at me. “So, young man, what seems to be the problem? I see here on your paperwork your side aches. Have a seat on the exam table and pull up your shirt. Let’s see what’s going on.”

Dr. Orback put the papers down as I sat on the exam table, but instead of lifting my shirt, I handed the doctor my card.

“I don’t really have a side ache, doc. I’m here on another matter.”

Dr. Orbach gazed at the card. “What’s this all about?” Bushy brown brows arched above hazel eyes.

“As you can see, I’m a private investigator from Palm Beach. A Della Carmichael, my client’s married name, hired me to look into her past. I don’t know why she can’t remember her earlier years, but she’s deathly afraid of doctors and hospitals, so finding the answers is challenging. I’ve tracked her former life here to Milton, but I know there’s more to the story. You’re my only connection to her early years, so I’ve come to see what you know about her.”

Dr. Orbach stared at me intently. I wasn’t sure whether he’d kick me out or help.

“I’ve never heard of Della Carmichael,” he finally said, offering no more explanation.

“What about a Della Smith, Della Brown, or Della Warren?”

Dr. Orbach shook his head. “Sorry. Don’t know anyone by those names either.”

“Perhaps you knew her by a different name—Della Wright?”

Dr. Orbach's eyes narrowed and twitched at the corners. He gave me an icy stare. "I'm afraid I can't help you. Let me show you out." He turned and walked toward the door.

"I know you know her," I said calmly but firmly. "And I know she was committed to Chattahoochee. What I don't know is why. What horrible deed did she commit that would land her in the mental hospital? And, who committed her?"

After hesitating, Dr. Orbach said, "Look, Mr. Marlow, you live far from Milton and Chattahoochee in a wealthy and largely populated area. You don't know what happens in small towns, and quite frankly, you don't want to. I suggest you return to Palm Beach and stop your investigation." He opened the door and waited for me to leave.

"I'll find out the truth, Dr. Orbach, with or without your help." I passed through the door, nodded to Miss Glass, and stomped out of the doctor's office toward Celia. Once inside, I took a deep breath and pounded the steering wheel with my fists. I'd come so far in time and distance only to be thwarted by the one person who knew Della and possibly had the answers. Why wouldn't he want to help Della uncover her past? What was he hiding?

About to start the car, I noticed a scrap of paper tucked beneath the wiper. Scrambling from my seat, I pulled out the note. The message, written in pencil, read: *Milton Methodist Church*.

I smiled, then looked up at the window in Dr. Orbach's office. A blind lowered, covering the face of the person standing there. I had been conflicted about my next move, but now I knew right where to go, thanks to Miss Glass.

Needing fuel, I pulled into the next gas station and asked the clerk how to find the church—"It's only a mile from here. Past the vacant pecan stand, turn north down the gravel road. You can't miss it."

Celia kicked up dust as we headed toward the church. Being a Monday, the place of worship was quiet, not a car in sight, yet a house, I presumed was the parsonage, sat about a half block away. Walking down the grassy path to the front porch, I noticed a large oak tree. Its huge leaf-filled branches shaded the house from the hot summer sun, and a swing with rope supports and a wooden seat dangled from a sizeable limb and rocked in the summer breeze.

After knocking on the door front door, a woman, who appeared around Della's age and so pregnant she looked as though she'd deliver any moment, answered. Her blonde, almost white hair arched around her oval face, and her pale blue eyes matched the color of her sleeveless dress.

"Hi, my name is Drake Marlow. I've driven up from Palm Beach and wondered if the pastor is in?"

"My husband, Pastor Walt, has gone into town just now, but please come in. You can wait for him. He shouldn't be too long. I'm his wife, Mrs. Billings, but everyone calls me Harriet." She held open the screen door for me to enter.

"Thank you, ma'am." The house was small but pleasantly decorated, with ample seating in the living room.

"How about a cup of coffee while you wait?" asked Harriet.

"I don't want to be a bother, ma'am."

"No bother. It's already made. Please sit down. I'll be back in a moment." She waddled through the adjacent dining room and into the kitchen, then returned, carrying a tray with two coffee cups, cream, and sugar balanced on her protruding belly. I jumped up, ready to help her, but she carefully set the tray on the coffee table in front of the couch.

"So, what brings you to Milton?" she asked, grabbing both arms of the chair opposite me and gingerly lowering herself.

I added a dab of cream and sugar to my coffee. "My friend and I are guests at the Middleton Farm while I conduct business in the area." I sipped the coffee; it tasted good.

"Oh, yes. Ron and Betty Middleton. They own the pecan orchard, right?"

"Yes, ma'am."

"Wonderful folks. We attend the pecan harvest festival every year. They're always so generous with their pecans. What kind of business are you in, Mr. Marlow?"

"Ah, it's a bit complicated, but suffice it to say I'm trying to locate information on a woman from Milton. Someone directed me to the church. This individual thought I'd find a connection between the church and this woman. I hoped your husband could help me."

"Perhaps I can help. I grew up in Milton and know just about everyone in town and then some. My papa was the pastor of this church until his health forced him to retire. Then he had a heart attack and passed. Mama passed not too long after that. My husband, Walt, and I met at church. It seems ironic that he became the pastor, I became his wife, and we now live in the same home I grew up in."

"Yes, ma'am."

"So tell me, Mr. Marlow, what's this person's name—the one you're looking for?" Harriet gazed wide-eyed at me and sipped her coffee.

I hesitated but figured she might have known Della since she'd grown up here and seemed about the same age.

Besides, what's the worst that could happen? She'd turn me out as the doctor did, and I'd be no closer or farther away from finding the answers.

"Her name is Della Wright."

Harriet's coffee cup slipped from her grasp, bounced off her belly, spilling coffee down her blue dress, and clattered onto the tray, breaking into pieces. She jumped up, pulling the dress away from her skin.

"I'll be right back," she said.

While Harriet was gone, I mopped the spilled coffee on the tray with our napkins and gathered the broken pieces of porcelain into a pile.

Harriet returned wearing a flower-print dress. She sat and gazed directly at me, her eyes saying it all.

"You know Della, don't you?" I asked, gazing back at her.

"We grew up together here in Milton," she said softly, radiating tenderness wrapped in memories. Tears formed in her eyes.

Excitement and compassion washed over me. "Please, Harriett, I need to know all about Della. What happened to her? Why was she sent to Chattahoochee?"

Harriet drew a hanky from her pocket and wiped her eyes. "It seems so long ago. Tell me how you know Della."

"I'm a private investigator. Della is my client. She's asked me to find out about her past as she doesn't seem to recollect any of it." I pulled a card from my wallet and handed it to Harriet.

She scrutinized the card.

"Wait here." She rose and left the room. When she returned, she carried a scrapbook and sat beside me on the couch. In silence, she opened the book and pointed to photos of two smiling little girls—one a towhead, the other with hair as dark as midnight. In one picture, Harriet sat on a swing, holding onto the ropes while Della stood beside her, draping an arm over her friend's shoulders. In the other, the girls sat at opposite ends of a teeter-totter.

"This is you and Della at the swing in the front yard," I said.

"Yes, when we were four. Della had just arrived at her Aunt Ginny's house, and her aunt wanted her to meet some children her age. I lived the closest, and as it turned out, we had birthdays two weeks apart. We became best friends and remained so until they took her away." Once again, Harriet dabbed at her tears.

"What happened?" I asked.

"It's a long story. First, let me tell you how Della came to live in Milton."

CHAPTER 26

"Wright is not Della's real last name. We don't know what it is. And Ginny was not her aunt. Again, we have no idea who her relatives were. Before Ginny's death, she told my father the real story. He told me. Dr. Orbach is the only other person who knows who Della really is."

I started to ask another question, but suddenly, Harriet doubled over and shrieked. She grabbed her belly and grimaced in pain.

"The baby! I think it's coming!"

"Now?" I asked, wide-eyed, my heart pumping.

"NOW!" she said, gritting her teeth against the agony of a contraction.

"Let's get you to the car. I'll drive you to Dr. Orbach's office."

"No. The contractions are coming too fast; I'll never make it down the steps. Labor is supposed to be longer than this, but I'm afraid the baby won't wait." Fear shone in her eyes as she gulped for air.

"What can I do?" I swallowed hard, hoping I didn't have to deliver the child myself.

"Call Dr. Orbach and ask him to come. His number is by the phone." Harriet's groans turned into wails.

I rushed to the phone. After relaying the message to Miss Glass, I helped Harriet to the bedroom, stacked pillows behind her, and brought a cool, damp washcloth for her perspiring forehead. The contractions continued, as did her wails. Helpless, I sat on the bed and held her hand, praying Dr. Orbach would make it here in time.

He did, along with Miss Glass.

~~~

The cry of a newborn permeated the house. Walt, who had arrived just minutes before, stopped his frantic pacing and extended a hand to me. He pumped mine like one would draw water from a well. "Thank God you were here. I don't know what would have happened if you hadn't been. I was only gone twenty minutes. I guess that's all it takes," he said.

"Glad I was here, too. Congratulations on becoming a father."

Walt dropped his hand and embraced me in a tight hug.

"It's a girl," said Dr. Orbach, poking his head into the living room. "Harriet's fine, and so is the baby. Congratulations, Walt." He walked over and shook the new father's hand.

"Can I see her—I mean them?" asked Walt excitedly.

"Let Miss Glass get the baby cleaned up first, then you can see them for just a few minutes. Harriet wants to see Mr. Marlow before he leaves." Dr. Orbach gazed at me as though that couldn't be fast enough.
~~~

"Of course," said Walt. He waited until Dr. Orbach returned to the living room, then bounded into the bedroom, leaving Dr. Orbach and me alone.

The doctor nodded toward the scrapbook on the couch, still open to photos of Harriet and Della. "I guess Harriet told you."

"Some of it, but not the whole story. I'd like to hear that from you."

"I'll tell you the rest when you're ready to leave. By the way, how did you know to come to the parsonage?"

"I told you I'd find the truth whether you helped me or not. As to who pointed me to the church, I never actually saw the person, so that will forever remain a mystery."

"Mr. Marlow, my wife asked to see you," said Walt.

I excused myself. Passing Miss Glass in the hallway, we nodded in unspoken understanding, and then I slipped into the bedroom where Harriet's new daughter suckled at her breast, discreetly covered by a light blanket.

"Mr. Marlow, it was God's divine plan that you were here. I don't know what would have happened if you hadn't been." Harriet smiled and gazed down at the baby.

"I have to say it's a first for me. I've never been remotely close to a delivery before."

"Perhaps it will prepare you for whenever your future wife gives birth. Now, let me tell you the rest of Della's story. Please sit."

I pulled out my pad and pen and sat in a chair beside the bed while Harriet continued her story.

"As I said, I don't know Della's birth name, but this is what Ginny told my father. Della's mother was raised by her father after her mother died when she was eight. A beautiful child, at age fourteen, someone raped her, and she became pregnant. Since her father was a prominent council member in their town and didn't want his daughter's situation to become public knowledge and upend his aspiring political career, he bribed a local judge to commit her to Chattahoochee. His daughter gave birth at age fifteen to Della in the hospital among the mentally ill."

I sat there numbed by this revelation and couldn't believe a father could do that to his daughter. Still, I'd heard stories of other young women and wives committed to Chattahoochee by their fathers and husbands for far less—smoking, sunbathing in the nude, overspending their allowance, and rebelling against the man of the house.

Harriet continued.

"After giving birth, it was agreed Della's mother could leave the hospital if she'd put the child up for adoption. Her father was prepared to make an excuse for his daughter's being away for so long, but he wouldn't accept the child. When Della's mother refused, her father kept her in the facility. Four years later, Della's mother contracted tuberculosis and died. That's when Della came to live with Ginny. She called herself Della's aunt, but she wasn't related. The grandfather paid Ginny to care for the child and keep her secret under the name of Della Wright. Ginny never knew who the grandfather was."

"I can't imagine what it must have been like for Della to be in that facility during her formative years with mentally ill patients and then to have her mother die. No wonder she is so deathly afraid of hospitals and doctors. You were her best friend. Did she ever say anything to you?"

"Della was shy when she first came to Milton, but over time she became just the opposite—overly outgoing. She was very popular with the boys and girls. All the while, she never spoke of her mother or her time in Chattahoochee. But she did wonder why others had fathers and grandparents, but she didn't."

"What happened after you graduated from high school?"

"One day, she simply disappeared. I never found out where she went or what happened to her. I tried, but everyone clammed up, including Ginny. I never heard from her again. My life continued, but I never forgot my best friend and prayed for her every night. Still do. Please, tell me about Della, Mr. Marlow."

I told Harriet everything I knew about her friend.

"I knew her early childhood was rough, but it seems her adult life has been rough, too." Harriet dabbed tears from her eyes and readjusted her sleeping child.

"Everyone seems to have controlled Della's life except her." I rose to go.

"Before you leave, Mr. Marlow, take one of the photos. When you see Della, please give it to her. Let her know Jesus loves her, that I love her, and think of her often. Tell her I'm here for her; our door is always open."

"I will, Harriet. She'll be glad to know you care. Thank you for your time."

"No, Mr. Marlow. Thank you. You've answered my prayers in so many ways." Harriet reached out her hand. I kissed the back of it before leaving.

"Oh, Mr. Marlow, one more thing."

I turned at the door. "Yes?"

"Please tell her no one will want to see her more than little Della." Harriet smiled and gazed at her sleeping pink-faced bundle.

Warmth like a bear hug engulfed me. I'd just witnessed the miracle of birth, the answer to many prayers, and the real meaning of friendship and love. My mother used to tell me there are no coincidences, just God's divine plan in action. I wasn't sure I believed that, but I couldn't argue with the result. Yet, there was still more to learn about Della's past before I could close this case.

I walked to the living room to exchange places with Walt and Miss Glass.

"Have a safe return trip, and God bless you," said Walt, giving me a final hug on his way to the bedroom.

"Ready to go?" asked Dr. Orbach.

"Just about, but you still owe me an explanation of what happened to Della." I went to the album, selected the photo of the girls at the swing, and placed it in my breast pocket.

"Let's sit on the porch," said the doctor. We both moved to the front porch, where we found two wooden rocking chairs.

The Milton physician sat silently, gazing out at the front yard for a prolonged period. He needed to speak first—the ball was in his court. I stared at the swing and imagined Della and Harriet as four-year-olds taking turns pushing each other. The girls had taken different paths into adulthood, yet I genuinely hoped they would reconnect somewhere down the line. I'm sure if they did, it would be as though no time had passed. True friendships were like that.

Finally, Dr. Orbach began.

"When Della was eighteen, she was ready to leave home. Before she did, she'd heard snippets of her past from Ginny but not enough to fill in all the blanks, so she demanded to know the full story. Ginny refused at first but felt so sorry for Della that she broke down and told her what had happened. Della insisted on meeting her grandfather, the man responsible for having her birthed in a mental institution and whom she blamed for killing her mother. When her grandfather got wind of her inquiries through intermediaries, he wouldn't hear of their meeting. By this time, he was a state representative. Having his past unearthed would require him to resign and send him packing from the political arena in disgrace, so once again, he bribed a judge to send Della back to Chattahoochee. Authorities took her from Ginny's home in the dead of night."

"What a horrible experience for Della! What happened to her after that? There has to be more to the story; otherwise, how'd she make it out of the hospital and down to Palm Beach?"

"I don't know, but a physician friend of mine works at the facility. Maybe he can help you. Only you cannot divulge his name or that of anyone who helps you obtain additional information. Do I have your word?"

"You do."

Dr. Orbach pulled a folded paper from his pocket and handed it to me.

"Thank you, doc." I stood and shook his hand. "Before I go, there's one more question I'd like to ask. How do you know so much about Della's past? What role did you play in her life?"

He gazed at me with unyielding eyes and swallowed hard. "I delivered Della at Chattahoochee."

"What? You worked at the hospital?"

"It was a long time ago, and I was on staff as a physician. Since it was the only hospital for miles, we delivered many babies. Most were from residents of the surrounding communities, but occasionally, a patient needed us."

"Then you know Della's mother's name."

"I only knew her first name—Kathryn. After discovering why and how Kathryn was committed to the facility, I resigned in disgust and moved to Milton, where I started my practice."

"You left Della and Kathryn there even though you knew she wasn't insane?"

Dr. Orbach threw up his hands and raised his raspy voice infused with defensiveness and frustration. "What could I do? The courts were in charge. They had the power."

I stared at him, unsure I fully understood any of this.

The doctor took a deep breath and exhaled. "After Della's mother died, *that* physician"—he pointed at the note he gave me—"contacted me to help arrange Della's care. I was the one who found Ginny and made arrangements with her. It's like I told you before. You don't want to know what goes on in a small town."

I left it at that and walked to my car.

Driving back to the Middleton Farm after what I'd just heard left me traumatized. I was deeply saddened by Della's background and beside myself with anger at her grandfather's treatment of her from childhood to adulthood. At least Dr. Orbach tried to help her when she was most vulnerable. Still, reflecting on a life with no say or control, no wonder Della sought to manipulate circumstances using the only tool she had—her body.

I reaffirmed my vow to find Della's despicable grandfather and discover the name of the man who sexually assaulted her mother.

CHAPTER 27

I was emotionally exhausted as I pulled into the driveway at the Middleton Farm in the late afternoon, and I was famished as well, not having eaten anything since breakfast. All I wanted to do was chomp down on something tasty and hit the hay, but I was a guest in someone else's home. I needed to keep my hunger and etiquette in check.

"I see you made it back," said Georganne, who greeted me at the front door. "But you look a little frazzled. Rough day?"

"You could say that."

"How about a bowl of soup and some sourdough bread? Dinner won't be ready for a few hours."

"You're an angel, Georganne. I haven't had anything since breakfast."

"Follow me," she said, crooking an index finger at me.

I sat at the kitchen table while she ladled soup into a bowl from a large pot on the stove, sliced several pieces of bread from the loaf, and set both before me, along with some butter and a glass of sweet tea. While I ate, she brought a bowl of green beans to the table and snapped them into a pot in preparation for the night's meal.

"I ran into a friend of yours today," I said, devouring the delicious chicken soup.

"Who's that?" *Snap. Snap.*

"Harriet Billings."

"Reverand Billings' wife? Isn't she precious? How is she? She's pregnant, and I haven't seen her for a while." *Snap.*

"She had her baby. A girl."

"You saw the child?" *Snap. Snap. Snap.*

"I practically delivered her."

Georganne abruptly stopped snapping. "Good heavens! What happened?"

For the next few minutes, I shared my experience at the Billings' home, leaving out sensitive information about Della.

"It sounds like the Lord put you there in the nick of time."

"Seems so. By the way, where are Ron and Cookie? I didn't see your husband's truck when I pulled in."

"Oh, they're still out touring the trees and the packing shed. They should be here any time. And I forgot to tell you, Betty Lou phoned. She asked that you call her back as soon as you return. She said it was very important."

"Excuse me, then. I'd better return the call." I went to the vestibule, where the phone sat on a sideboard, and reversed the call so the Billings wouldn't incur any long-distance charges.

Betty Lou answered on the first ring.

"It's me. Georganne said you had important news."

"Do I! Willie was able to locate Bluto. He's not in custody yet, but Chief Borman is on his heels, so it won't be long now. You might want to cut your trip short and get back here."

"Can't right now," I said, lowering my voice. "I found people who know Della. It isn't a pretty story."

"Care to enlighten?"

"Not yet. I'm following up on leads and heading to Chattahoochee tomorrow."

"You're going to the looney bin? Alone?"

"That's where I hope to wrap up this case."

"Okay, Boss, but be careful. I've heard strange things happen to people who go snooping around up there. Have you got Marvin with you?"

"Yep. He'll be my constant companion."

"One more thing before I hang up," said Betty Lou. "Mrs. Carmichael called. She said she was still out of town but wanted to check in and get an update on the progress."

"What did you tell her?"

"I told her you were out of town, too, making inquiries. She said she would return next week and see you then."

"Thanks, Betty Lou. I'll phone you tomorrow when I get back from the hospital. I'll have a lot to tell you then.

Ron, Cookie, and Bill entered the house as I hung up. We chatted a bit, and then I went upstairs to lie down for an hour before dinner.

Georganne served an excellent meal, and Cookie shared an animated tale of his trip to the pecan orchard and packing house. I told them about meeting Harriet, her pastor husband, and being there for their daughter's birth. After dinner, we sat on the porch and made peach ice cream in a hand-cranked churn.

"I know there's more to the story than what you told us at dinner," said Cookie once we returned to our room.

"There's a lot more, my friend, but I won't know the entire story until tomorrow after my visit to Chattahoochee." I sat on the bed and took off my shoes and socks.

"Blimey, mate! Why are you goin' there?" Cookie stood, hands on hips, with a penetrating stare.

"I'm told that's where I'll find the rest of the story." I undressed and put on my pajamas.

"Yeah, but aren't you scared?"

"I'll have Marvin with me." I slipped under the covers.

"That may be, but what if they search you before you can enter? They'll find Marvin; he won't do you any good once you're inside."

I turned over and feigned sleep, ending our conversation. I knew what Cookie said was true, but I was going to Chattahoochee tomorrow, and no one was going to stop me, even with tales of possible pat-downs.

~~~

The trip took me a few hours, retracing my drive east along SR 1 toward Chattahoochee. The first landmark I saw was a lofty water tower with "Florida State Hospital" painted in blue, indicating I'd reached my destination. The second was the majestic white administrative building at the entrance to the massive compound, much of it enclosed by chain-linked fencing. I climbed the broad steps of the large building and admired the masterfully carved cornices along the roofline and the ornate front porch railing. Inside, a receptionist greeted me.

"What patient are you here to see?" asked a plain-looking woman around my age.
~~~

"No, no. I'm not here to see a patient. I'm Drake T. Marlow from Palm Beach, Florida. I'm here to see Dr. Norman Sieler." I handed her my card.

She eyeballed me skeptically. "Do you have an appointment?"

"No, but when you call him, please let him know I'm here on a referral from Dr. Orbach."

"Please wait. I'll see if Dr. Sieler is available." She picked up the receiver, dialed a number, and explained who I was and my request. "He's with a patient, but his assistant will be here in about thirty minutes to get you. You can have a seat." She gestured at the reception room dotted with visitors.

I sat in a worn wooden chair in a small seating area in one corner of the expansive room and studied the building. A wooden structure that looked decades old, the interior could have used a fresh coat of paint. Several visitors came and went as they checked in and were escorted by white-coated orderlies to meet their friend or relative. Several magazines—*Time, Life, True Confessions, Detective*—lay on a coffee table in front of me. I picked up *Detective* and began to read, trying to learn something new about my profession. I didn't get far.

"Excuse me. Are you here to see someone?"

I gazed up to find an aged gentleman supporting himself on a cane standing before me. He looked none too steady. "Yes," I said.

"I'm Dr. Wilson. Perhaps I could help." He pointed to his name embroidered above the pocket of a white doctor's coat.

"Drake T. Marlow," I said, standing and introducing myself. "I'm waiting for Dr. Sieler."

"Ah, yes. The head medical doctor. He's a fine gentleman. Been here a long time, but not as long as me." The elderly doctor, thin and frail, winked a hazel eye.

"How long have you been here?"

"Oh, my. It seems like forever. A last count, I think it was thirty-seven years."

Longer than I'd been alive!

"May I sit?" he asked.

"Of course." I gestured to the chair beside me. "It seems like this facility has been here a long time too. I'd love to know a bit of its history."

Dr. Wilson gingerly lowered himself into the chair and placed his cane between his legs. He rested his hands on the crooked end, exposing one of his wrists encircled by a thin band of braided threads. The piece was filthy and looked like he hadn't taken it off or washed it for decades.

"History?" he asked. "You've come to the right place for that, young man. What would you like to know?"

"Everything," I said. I had thirty minutes to kill.

Dr. Wilson pulled back, then reversed course and leaned in. He spoke just above a whisper. "Oh, I can't tell you everything, Mr. Marlow. That would be divulging too many secrets. Let's just stick to its history, shall we?" His toothy grin exposed tobacco-stained teeth as he sat back.

I couldn't tell if he was serious or kidding. Most likely, these walls had seen their share of dark secrets, and I wouldn't be surprised if the old doctor knew most of them, but did he know Della's secrets? If so, could I coax them out of him?

"Very well. Tell me its history." I settled in for an informative lecture, though my ulterior motive was to steer him toward Della's story.

"You see," he said, "these buildings began as a fort to store munitions during the Second Seminole War when the buildings were known as the Apalachicola Arsenal. And this building was originally the officer's quarters. The U.S. government waged three wars against the Seminole Indians to remove them from Florida land so settlers could move in. But, of course, the Indians never really left. They merely ran into the Everglades where they holed up."

"I studied the wars in school, and the Seminoles still live in the Everglades. I've met some," I said proudly.

"You don't say!" Crooked lines creased the surprised doctor's brow. "I'd like to meet them. Wouldn't that be exciting?" He clapped his palms together like a child.

"You're invited to come down any time. I'll introduce you." At this gentleman's age—I guessed in the late seventies—I didn't expect him to make the trip south, but I wanted him to feel welcome just the same.

Dr. Wilson continued, giving me a rundown on the long history of the Florida State Hospital, from an arsenal during the Seminole and Civil wars to Florida's first state prison to the Florida Asylum for the Indigent Insane. He included stories of daring escapes, changes in staff and administrators, inspections, and treatment. The doctor even told me of a patient called "the old metal eater" who ate metal objects, including silverware, wood, and paper. The older man's memory was remarkable, and the fascinating stories mesmerized me, but what I really wanted to know was if he'd known Della.

I decided to take a chance and plunged ahead.

"By any chance, would you have known a young girl named Kathryn? She gave birth to a little girl named Della, who grew up here until she was about four. This would have been some time back—maybe thirty years ago."

"Mmm," said Dr. Wilson, brushing a hand over his whiskered chin as though deep in thought. "As I recall, Kathryn died of tuberculosis. She was a beautiful young woman and a lovely person. And her daughter? You could tell the child would be stunning even at a young age."

My heart lept at his recognition. I leaned forward, my whole body stiffening. "So, you knew them."

"Of course. Kathryn and I spoke daily, and she told me about what had happened and how she wound up here. She cried a lot, wanting to go home. I tried to help her, but I had no power to discharge her. After her daughter was born, she stopped crying, wanting to be strong and protective of her child."

"Can you tell me more?" I asked.

"Her daughter was a very sweet and loving child. I did everything I could to teach her about nature, the alphabet, and her numbers. She often called me Papa, and my heart broke when she asked me where her real papa was. The day after Kathryn died, Della left the facility. I never saw her again." A sadness fell over Dr. Wilson like a dark veil. He dropped his head and gazed at the floor as though remembering that very day brought a surge of pain.

“I can tell you this, Dr. Wilson, Della was placed in a very loving household and grew up among great friends. She’s grown into quite the woman.” I wasn’t about to tell him her sad story.

“I’m so happy to hear that.” A smile returned to the doctor’s face.

“By any chance, do you remember the name of the man Kathryn said was Della’s father?”

“I do,” he said. “It’s—”

But Dr. Wilson never finished the sentence because, just then, two men in white coats approached.

“We’ve been looking for you,” said the taller man staring at Dr. Wilson.

“Going back to your office to see your patients?” I asked.

The doctor gave me a sheepish look.

“More like he’s going back to the ward,” said the shorter man with a laugh. “Dr. Wilson lives here and evades the orderlies from time to time.”

I looked at the men wide-eyed. “You mean he isn’t a doctor?”

“Oh, he’s a doctor, alright—a Ph.D. in history and used to teach at the Florida State College for Women. He fooled you, right? Just like all the others. Take my advice, friend, don’t believe a word he tells you.”

I glared at Dr. Wilson in disbelief.

“C’mon, Dr. Wilson, let’s get you back to the ward,” the taller man said.

The two men lifted Dr. Wilson from his chair and were about to lead him out of the building when he stretched his hand back.

"Please give this to Della. She'll know what it is." He dropped something into my hand and gave me a parting smile.

I watched Dr. Wilson shuffle between the two men and out the door. Stunned and at a loss for words, I opened my hand. Curled in my palm lay the dirty thread bracelet. I had no idea of its significance, but I was sure the discolored threads would evoke meaningful memories for Della.

CHAPTER 28

A tall woman in street clothes approached within minutes of Dr. Wilson's exit. "Mr. Marlow, Dr. Sieler will see you now. Please follow me."

She led me without conversation out the back of the building, across a sizeable courtyard crisscrossed by concrete sidewalks, and toward a three-story building. Climbing the wide stairs, she produced a key and unlocked a door. We headed down a long corridor before stopping at room 135. Inside was a reception area.

"Please have a seat." She disappeared behind a closed door. Seconds later, she emerged. "Dr. Sieler will see you now." She held the door open for me to enter.

On the other side was another office with two chairs in front of a well-worn desk. Behind it, bookshelves stuffed with medical books lined the wall. A bespectacled, balding man sporting a salt and pepper beard and goatee sat behind the desk. He gestured for me to sit.

"I understand you know my old friend Dr. Orbach. I haven't seen him in a while, but we often correspond. I hope he's well." Dr. Sieler gave me a friendly smile though he didn't offer a handshake.

"Yes, he's fine. He spoke highly of you." I withdrew a calling card from my wallet and handed it to Dr. Sieler. I let the information soak in a moment before I spoke. "Thank you for seeing me on such short notice. As you can see, I'm Drake Marlow, a private investigator from Palm Beach. I hope you can help me with a case I'm working on."

"I'll do what I can." He placed my card on his desk.

"This has to do with a former patient of yours."

"And the person's name?"

"Della Wright."

The doctor stiffened and stared at me without blinking as though time had stopped.

"Look," I said, leaning forward and speaking softly. "I understand this is a sensitive issue, but Della's mental health hangs in the balance. She's my client and has asked me to find out who she is. I've traced her back to this institution. I know what happened to her mother, Kathryn, why she was sent to the hospital, and that Della was born here. I also know how you, with Dr. Orbach's help, arranged for her at age four to live with Ginny after her mother died. And I know someone sent her back to the hospital when she was eighteen."

Dr. Sieler blinked. His Adam's apple traveled up and down as he swallowed multiple times.

"I'd like to know her real last name and why she was removed from her home in the dead of night and returned to the hospital after graduation. I'd also like to know how she eventually made it out of the hospital. I was told you could help me." I stared at Dr. Sieler, hoping I hadn't pushed too hard too fast.

The doctor's brow puckered, and his eyes narrowed. Beads of sweat broke out on his forehead. He dabbed at the moisture with a handkerchief. "That was a long time ago. The parties involved in those decisions are still alive and prominent government figures wielding immense power. What you're trying to do will open Pandora's Box!"

"Were these prominent persons patients of yours?"

"No," he said, drawing out the word as though questioning where this conversation was heading.

"But Della was. And, in a way, she still is. Isn't your first obligation to your patients? Oh, she may not currently reside in the hospital, but she lives in the darkness of her experience here. As a physician, isn't your job to help your patients heal? To help Della heal?"

Dr. Sieler closed his eyes and shook his head. "I want to help, but you don't understand. This situation is very complicated."

"I understand you once assisted a helpless child escape her hopeless life here. Now I'm asking you to do it again. Della's still that child, only in a woman's body. With your help, hopefully, she can shed that child and become the healthy woman she was meant to be."

The doctor combed his hands through what was left of his hair. He placed his elbows on the desk, steepled his fingers, and rested his chin on them. “I need time to think.”

“With all due respect, doc, time is running out. I’ll find the answer with or without your help, and when I do, the people you’re protecting will wonder where it came from. Whether you supply the information or not, in all likelihood, those people will believe the finger points to you.” I emphasized my accusation by jabbing a finger in his direction.

“I need time!” he said, pounding the desk with his fists.

“I’ll be at this telephone number until tomorrow. Then I’m off to my next stop in the investigation.” I wrote the Middletons’ phone number on the back of my calling card. “I hope to hear from you before I leave.”

Dr. Sieler’s secretary escorted me out of the building. I walked across the courtyard, back through the Administration Building, and headed to the parking lot. My time with Dr. Sieler had been a total bust, with my optimism and enthusiasm for this case hitting an all-time low. I had no clue where I’d go from here, so I sat in Celia and considered my options.

How would I discover Della’s last name and what happened to her without his help? I racked my brain to filter through all I knew about her. She was twenty-eight now, so she was born in 1904 or 1905. And what had Harriet told me? Their birthdays were two weeks apart. If I contacted Harriet and asked her for her birthdate, perhaps she’d remember Della’s, or at least if it was before or after hers.

With that information, I could search birth certificates for that four-week time frame and cross-reference the dates with the mother's name—Kathryn, and the place of delivery—Florida State Hospital. How many Kathryns would have given birth within that window in that institution in Gadsden County? If I could find the correct document, it would tell me Della's last name and perhaps that of her father, her mother's rapist.

The state repository for all birth and death certificates and marriage licenses was the Bureau of Vital Statistics under the direction of the State Board of Health in Jacksonville. I was sure I'd find a wealth of information there, including Della's marriage license to her first husband, under the last name of Warren, and his death certificate, indicating the cause. I'd also find information on her second marriage to Stanley Carmichael. I needed to get to the repository, but first, I'd return to the Middleton farm, where I'd stay the night before leaving for Jacksonville in the morning with Cookie.

I stopped for lunch at a roadside diner and phoned the Billings; Walt answered. Harriet and little Della were doing well, with their icebox overflowing with food and their home awash in gifts from their wonderful friends and neighbors. Harriet said her birthday was October 5, 1905, but she couldn't remember Della's actual birthday, though it was close to hers. Because of that, the girls always celebrated between the two dates. Harriet recalled the party was typically held after her birthday, suggesting Della's birthday was on or before October 19. This more compact time frame would result in a shorter search.

Once I reached the farm, I called Betty Lou, dictated an update, and asked her to type up the notes and insert them into Della's file. If something happened to me, I wanted documentation of my investigation and what I'd found. After that, I told the Middletons that Cookie and I would head to Jacksonville tomorrow and couldn't thank them enough for their hospitality.

We ate Betty's delicious beef stew, buttery biscuits, corn on the cob, and greens. Chocolate pecan pie—a gift from heaven—completed the meal. Then we enjoyed our last night with the family talking and playing games. They were curious about what I'd found on my trip, but naturally, I couldn't tell them since I needed to keep everything confidential. Perhaps when the case was over, I'd share my experience. Until then, I had to keep my lips buttoned.

After a full day, I was thankful to crawl between the cool sheets and close my eyes. But just as I was about to enter blissful sleep, a muted knock on the bedroom door awakened me.

"Drake, it's Ron," he whispered, trying not to wake Cookie or the whole household. "I need to speak with you."

I stumbled out the bedroom door and into the hall in a foggy state. "What is it? Is the family okay?" I blinked and scrubbed my face, trying to clear my eyes and head of sleep.

"They're fine. Dr. Orbach is on the phone for you. He says it's urgent and sounds most upset."

"I'll be right down." I pulled on pants and a shirt and trudged downstairs. When I picked up the receiver, Ron slipped into the kitchen to give me privacy.

"This is Drake Marlow," I said, trying to sound awake.

"Dr. Sieler is dead. They found a syringe nearby containing remnants of a powerful tranquilizer. Given enough, it would stop a man's heart. The police don't know if it was murder or suicide."

My mouth fell open as I caught my breath, and I swayed slightly, catching myself against the cabinet. Did Dr. Orbach think I had something to do with the Chattahoochee doctor's death?

"I swear he was alive when I left."

"What did you talk about?" His tone reeked of controlled anger.

"I merely told Dr. Sieler what I knew and asked for his help. He was afraid to give me Kathryn's last name because if it became public, her father would conclude the information came from him. He feared this person, saying the man wielded great power. The doctor wanted time to think."

"Your card was found in his pocket with the Middletons' phone number. You must have given it to him. Why?"

I gulped. "I wanted Dr. Sieler to reconsider his answer and gave him the Middletons' phone number so if he did, he could reach me before I returned to Palm Beach."

"That's all you said?" asked Orbach.

"I might have said if he didn't provide the information, I'd get it another way, but the onus of the information would probably fall on him either way." I closed my eyes against the chastisement I knew was coming.

"So you threatened him?" Dr. Orbach said sternly.

"I wanted him to do the right thing and help Della. After all, she was his patient and needed to know the truth. Her future well-being depended on it."

"The police are looking for you and will be at the Middleton's soon. I suggest you leave now unless you want to spend a considerable portion of your future in Chattahoochee." He hung up.

Ron came out of the kitchen. He saw the panic on my face. "What's going on?"

"Cookie and I need to leave. And you may get a visit from the police. The man I spoke with earlier today is dead. They may think I had something to do with it. I didn't. Don't lie to the police, but don't tell them everything, either. And as far as you're concerned, we left, and you have no idea where we're headed. Thank you for your hospitality." I turned and ascended the stairs two at a time.

I woke Cookie, and we tossed our belongings haphazardly into our suitcases and climbed into Celia in record time. Ron caught us in the driveway just before we pulled out to give us a final goodbye and a box of food and water.

Exhausted from the day's events yet with adrenalin pumping, I drove east, explaining our abrupt departure to Cookie. About five miles east of the Middletons, we passed a police car speeding in the opposite direction. I was sure they were heading for the farm. After driving another three hours, we found lodging on the outskirts of Tallahassee and dragged ourselves into our room. At 2:30 a.m., we collapsed onto the beds and fell fast asleep.

~~~

I jerked upright, and my heart leaped to my throat at the sound of someone pounding on the door. With a tightening chest, I eyeballed Cookie. Had the police found us already?

"Mr. Marlow, this is the front desk clerk with your wake-up call. It's eight o'clock."

"Thank you," I managed to eke out, realizing the morning had come way too soon. I tried calming my racing heart by taking a deep breath and exhaling slowly.

"Crikey!" said Cookie, gazing at me. "When I suggested we go on a road trip, this wasn't exactly what I had in mind."

"Come on and get dressed. We'll grab breakfast and head to Jacksonville before the police catch up to us."

After quickly dressing, Cookie and I entered the little café across the street. He ordered two boxed breakfasts while I called Betty Lou from their pay phone. I told her what had happened and that we were heading to Jacksonville.

"Since the police found my card in the doctor's pants, you'll probably get a call from them. They'll want to know where I am and why I visited Dr. Sieler."

"Don't worry, Boss, I can handle them." Betty Lou wanted to stay strong, but I could tell by her shaking voice she was concerned. "You still have Marvin?"

"I do."

"Please don't use him."
~~~

"This isn't the Old West," I said, trying to make light of the situation.

"Yeah, I know. But one never knows how they'll react if cornered."

"Don't worry about me. Please phone Chief Borman and tell him what's happened. Since he knows Della's case and my character, you have my permission to fill him in on everything that's happened. Perhaps he can run interference if things get dicey. Any update on Bluto?"

"Not yet, but the chief says he's so close they can smell the big guy. He's optimistic they'll cuff him soon."

"That's encouraging."

Cookie motioned to me he had the breakfasts and it was time to leave.

"I've got to go, but don't forget to call Borman."

"Will do, and Godspeed," said Betty Lou.

Cookie and I headed east once again. During the next hour, I explained to him what we'd be looking for once we arrived at the government building. His help combing through hundreds of documents would save considerable time. Still, my concern was that once he learned the truth about Della, whatever that was, it would negatively impact his opinion of her.

Mired in an emotional stew of uncertainty about what we'd find, I drove into the heart of Jacksonville after four hours on the road. As navigator, Cookie used a local map to guide me down numerous narrow streets until I pulled into a parking lot on Springfield Blvd., abutting a residential neighborhood. The lettering outside the building stated: State Board of Health. Knowing that what I was about to uncover would impact others' lives forever, for good or ill, my heart quickened as I stared at the expansive building built atop a mound.

"This is it," I said, strengthening my resolve to finish this case.

"No worries, mate," said Cookie, smiling. Then, with a fist thrust into the air and the rallying cry of a committed combatant heading into battle, he bellowed, "Let's get in there, open Pandora's Box, and free Della!"

Long strides affirmed our determination as Cookie and I marched side-by-side like ardent warriors toward the building and up the steps.

CHAPTER 29

An extensive directory indicating floor and suite numbers of the various services occupying the State Board of Health offices greeted us. The Division of Public Health Nursing, Bureau of Communicative Diseases, Bureau of Laboratories, Bureau of Sanitary Engineering, and Bureau of Vital Statics were among them. The office we wanted was to our right, down a long corridor. As we entered the office, a counter separated the reception and work areas, where a dozen clerks sat at desks typing away.

"May I help you?" asked a woman about my age—sandy hair, deep blue eyes, Gina on her nametag.

"You may," I said, handing her my card and lowering my voice just above a whisper. "I'm working on a very hush-hush case and need to view a birth certificate from 1905."

"Hmm. That was a long time ago. Have you checked the courthouse in the county of the person's birth?" Gina looked between Cookie and me.

"I thought the state stored birth, death, marriage, and divorce documents here," I said.

"They do, but the state didn't require counties to send those records here until 1915. Of course, the counties have been sending us copies of all their documents before that time, but that doesn't mean we have all of them. If we do, they'd be in the basement."

"The basement? I didn't think buildings in Florida had basements because of the high water table."

"Well, several homes in the city have them, and this building has one because they built it on a mound. The records for the year you're asking about are down there. If you fill out this request form, we'll get back to you when we've located it."

"Great," I said, accepting the form. "And how long will that take?"

"Could be a month or so," she said, delivering the shocking news with a straight face.

"A month!?" I blinked in disbelief.

"Mr. Marlow, we don't go down there that often. Only when someone requests an old document."

"I don't think you understand, Gina. We're only looking for certificates within a two-week time frame. How difficult could that be?"

With fists stuck on her hips, Gina's eyes narrowed. "You're the one who doesn't understand, Mr. Marlow. Once we're down there, searching the files and finding the information takes time. Do you have any idea how many records we have to sort through?"

I chuckled. "There couldn't have been that many births in Florida in 1905."

Gina smirked. She reached into a drawer and pulled out a paper. Drawing her finger down a typed report, she stopped about halfway. "According to the Bureau of Vital Statistics annual report, there were 27,204 births in the state in 1905." She turned the paper toward me so that I could see the figure.

"But Gina, this is an urgent matter. A woman's life hangs by a thread without this information. We need it today."

"Unless law enforcement requests priority, you'll have to wait until we have time to sort through the records," she said sternly.

"Is this typical of the kind of service this office provides its Florida citizens? If so, perhaps you're overpaid," I huffed in frustration.

Cookie gasped behind me.

"On second thought, Mr. Marlow, I apologize. I may have given you the wrong information on how long this process would take."

"Well, I'm glad you've come to your senses." I beamed and gave myself an unseen congratulatory pat on the back.

"Yes, sir. I definitely was mistaken. The information you request may take more like two months to find." She raised her hand, displaying two fingers. A smirk wandered her lips.

I wanted to strangle her.

"Is there a pay phone in the building?"

"Down the hall before you get to the restrooms." Gina pointed to her left.

"Fine. Come on, Cookie. I'll call Chief Borman. He'll put in the request for us." Though Gina had won the battle, the war wasn't over. Cookie and I walked out of the office and headed for the phone.

While I picked up the receiver to call the chief, Cookie walked toward the restroom.

"Yes, operator, please connect me with Police Chief Joseph Borman in Palm—" I didn't have time to finish my sentence because Cookie depressed the phone's cradle, cutting me off.

"What are you doing?" I asked, annoyed at his gesture.

"Shhh," he said, putting an index finger to his lips. He beckoned me to follow.

About ten feet past the restrooms, he pointed to a door with a gold inscription: *Basement, Employees Only*. Cookie gazed at me, smiled, and jerked his thumb toward the door.

"No!" I said, shaking my head.

"That word never stopped us before." Cookie tried the door. Unlocked. "Come on," he said, grabbing my shirt and yanking me inside before I could offer a second protest.

The air temperature was cooler than that of the building but musty and stagnant as we stood motionless on a landing, letting our eyes get used to the utter darkness.

"Try the wall. There has to be a light switch somewhere," said Cookie.

I groped along one wall; he the other.

Light!

As we descended the stairs into the bowels of the building, the basement opened into a vast one-story space lighted by bare bulbs. Filling the chamber was a sea of wooden and mental file cabinets, card catalogs, and an assortment of old furniture and lab equipment. Walking down the central aisle, we realized the expanse had been sectioned off, with each department having its own area.

"All we have to do is find the Bureau of Vital Statistics space and start looking," said Cookie.

I was torn. My ethical instinct and reputation reminded me this wasn't a good idea. My investigative intuition and the situation's urgency told me to go for it. After all, didn't Gina say no one went into the basement that often? It wasn't like we were breaking and entering; the door was unlocked. But we were trespassing in a government building. At minimum, that would be a misdemeanor. Did I want to risk a criminal charge? I reasoned once we found the 1905 file cabinets, we'd only have to look in the files between May 5 and May 19. That shouldn't take too long.

"I'm in, but we have to work quickly. If we don't find the certificate within a reasonable length of time, we leave. Okay?"

"Okay, mate."

We located the Bureau of Vital Statistics section several minutes later and the three four-drawer file cabinets from 1905. We stood there, staring at them, wondering what they might hold.

"After you," said Cookie, stretching his hand toward the first file cabinet.

Minutes away from success, my fingers tingled as I grabbed the handle and pushed the latch to open the first file drawer. Countless folders stuffed to the gills with documents stared back at me. As I fingered through them, I let out an expletive.

"What's the matter, mate?" asked Cookie, gazing over my shoulder.

"The records aren't filed by date or county. They're filed alphabetically by last name!" I combed my fingers through my hair in exasperation. "Since we don't know Della's real last name, we'll have to review every document. That will take us hours, maybe days, to go through twenty-seven thousand birth certificates."

"We'd better get started then," said Cookie, the eternal optimist.

Knowing the risk if we got caught, yet realizing what was at stake for Della, I acquiesced. We pulled several old chairs from the pile of used office equipment and brought them into our aisle so we could sit on two and use the other two as makeshift tables. Then, we vigorously attacked our mission behind the wall of file cabinets.

With Cookie taking one cabinet and me another, we started with the top drawers and pulled out a file folder, scanning each document to see if it fell within our target dates. If it did, we'd cross-reference the certificate with the place of birth—Gadsden County—the mother's name—

Kathryn, and the physician's name—Dr. Orbach. When one criterion didn't match, we returned the document to the folder and went to the following certificate.

Scanning for the first criterion would have been relatively easy had the certificates been typed, but most of these documents were handwritten. Deciphering handwriting and smudged entries was challenging, especially without a magnifying glass. Besides, many of these documents were old and brittle, some even falling apart, though we did our best to keep them intact. After two hours, we'd only covered about half a drawer apiece.

"This is impossible," I said, slamming a file onto the chair. Its contents promptly flew out, landing haphazardly on the concrete floor. I let out another expletive.

"Come on, mate. We'll find it," said Cookie, giving me an encouraging pat on my back.

Cookie continued to sort through his papers while I picked up the scattered documents and placed them as best I could back into the folder. After considerable time, we still hadn't found Della's birth certificate and barely covered a drawer apiece.

"Is someone down there? I'm locking up," a man called from the stairs.

Cookie and I stiffened and eyeballed each other. Had we been here that long? I looked at my watch—6:00 p.m.

"Okay, then," said the man.

Suddenly, we were plunged into darkness as he turned off the light and closed the basement door. I waited about thirty seconds, then lit a match.

"Now what?" I asked in the flickering glow.

"Well, mate, you wanted time to review the files; now you have it. Be careful what you wish for."

"Yeah, but it's Friday night! Tomorrow's the weekend. What about food? A bed? Sleep?"

Cookie looked around and shrugged. "The chairs and floor are hard, but the situation could be worse."

"Worse?"

"Yeah. You remember France, don't you? Rain, muddy tents, bullets flying?"

"You have a point, but we can't stay here all weekend. I'm going to see if we can get out of here." I blew out the match, whose flame was down to my fingers, and lit another one. We started for the stairs.

Extinguishing the match at the landing, I gingerly opened the door and peered out. All was quiet—no sign of a soul anywhere. Our first stop was the restroom across the hall. After that, we walked the corridors, trying each outside door to see if any were open. They weren't, and each required a key to open from the inside—so much for dinner, a late-night snack, or a soft bed.

As we made our way back to the basement, we stumbled upon the employee lunchroom. Cookie made a beeline for the ice box.

"Hey, I found some carrots and a half-eaten sandwich. Want any?" asked Cookie.

"I'll take the carrots; you can have the sandwich," I said, scrunching my nose at the leftovers.

After peeling back the bread and sniffing the sandwich's contents—chicken salad—Cookie devoured his dinner in two bites. A hall drinking fountain provided water.

"Okay. Back to our search," said Cookie.

We wandered back down the corridor and through the basement door, where we turned on the light. Sitting in our cubby, we began perusing the documents once again. Hours later, we had finished only four drawers between us. After examining hundreds of additional documents, several more trips to the restroom, and numerous stretches, I needed a break.

"I don't think I can look at one more certificate. My eyes are tired, and my back aches."

"Why don't you lean back and take a nap, mate? I still have a couple of hours left in me, so I'll keep goin'." Cookie closed one drawer, opened another, and withdrew the next folder.

I leaned back, balancing the chair on the two legs, and closed my eyes.

~~~

Awaking with a jerk and a thud as the legs of my chair hit the floor, darkness enveloped me like a bad dream. Once I oriented myself, I pulled out my matches and lit one, only to find Cookie gone, and the time 4:20 a.m. Massaging my neck, partially paralyzed from my awkward nap, I moved to the stairs and the landing. Blowing out the match, I opened the door. When we had walked the hallways earlier, windows and doors allowed outside light to infuse the corridors and open spaces with light, allowing us to see where we were going. Now, though, night had arrived, and nothing but darkness permeated the building.

Closing the door, I flicked on the basement light and went back downstairs, returning with a chair to wedge the
~~~

door open so the basement light could shine into the hallway. Now that I could see, I walked to the lobby.

"Cookie?" My voice reverberated through the open area, then dissipated. I tried again. No response.

Had he found more comfortable sleeping arrangements in an office somewhere? More dinner? The building had three floors, and I was uncomfortable looking through every office for him. Besides, I'd be taking time valuable time away from the research. In addition to Della's birth certificate, I wanted to find her marriage licenses under the names Carmichael and Warren. Cookie knew where I was, so I'd just have to wait until he returned. In the meantime, I'd continue my search.

On my way back to the basement, I fingered the recesses of my mind to remember what I'd learned in survival training in the Army. One can live over thirty days without food but only three without water. Thankfully, we had water, so in the worst case, we'd have to wait until Monday to leave when workers returned and opened the building. We'd be famished, of course, but we'd be alive and hopefully have the desperately needed information.

When I returned to our workspace, I noticed all the drawers in Cookie's file cabinet were closed, with no files on the chair. Did that mean he'd found Della's certificate or finished his cabinet? The latter, I surmised; otherwise, I'm sure he would have awakened me to shout the good news. And so I continued to sort through the documents in my file cabinet.

Hours passed, but I found only a nibble or two—dates that matched and even the county, but not the mother's name or Dr. Orbach's. I continued my search.

The sound of the basement door opening startled me.

Cookie?

I cautiously peered over the cabinets to see a man in a hat poking his head through the door. "This is Brinks Security. Anyone down there?" The man waited a moment, then moved onto the landing. A shorter, second man joined him.

I held my breath, afraid to even breathe. My heart pounded in my ears.

"It's probably nothing, and someone simply left the light on, but we should probably take a look anyway just to be sure," the shorter man said.

As quietly as possible, I replaced the file folders in the cabinet and closed the drawer. I couldn't do anything about removing the chairs, but I could evade the officers by maneuvering down the aisles and between the sections as they moved in my direction.

"See anything, Joe?"

"Nothing down these aisles," Joe chuckled. "Maybe old Mrs. Pickett was hallucinating again when she reported seeing lights coming from the building while walking her dog."

"Could be, but the lights couldn't have been coming from the basement, so why are they on? Hey, what's this? There are chairs in the aisle like someone was using them to sort through the file cabinets. I'm going to take a look."

A lump formed in my throat as I kept low and sneaked around the cabinets like a mouse evading two cats. Though I couldn't see the men, I could hear them move down the aisle.

"The chairs are in front of the file cabinets from 1905. Maybe one of the clerks had an assignment and left the lights on. I'll have to ask Gina if she knows who was looking into files from that year."

"Well, I don't see anyone down here, and nothing else looks out of place. Let's go," said Joe.

The security officers walked back up the stairs and took a final look into the basement from the landing before switching off the light.

I stood motionless, hoping my rapidly beating heart would return to normal. The door opened again two minutes later, and the light came on. This time Cookie stood on the landing. He scrambled down the stairs and returned to the aisle where we were working. I made my way back there, too.

"Where have you been?" I asked, both curious and annoyed.

"I don't have time to explain. We need to get out of here," said Cookie, grabbing my arm. Heading for the stairs, he pulled me behind him.

"But what about the files? What about Della?" I glanced back with longing at our chairs and the file cabinets.

"If you want to leave the building, now is the time. The security officers have gone up to the second floor, and the front door is unlocked. Come on!" He started for the stairs. I followed.

Cookie turned off the light at the landing and cracked the door open. Muted early morning light filtered into the hallway, allowing us to see where we were going. Cookie moved into the corridor with me behind him, stepping as carefully and silently as possible. Arriving at the foyer, we took one last look around and listened intently before exiting the building.

Once outside, we raced down the steps and made a run for the parking lot. We were almost to Celia when someone yelled, "There they are!"

I turned to see the Brink's men leaning out a second-floor window, pointing at us. Just as I reached Celia, I saw the two security officers running full speed toward us. Cookie and I scrambled into our seats. I started the engine and jammed the shift into first. The officers were too far away to catch us as we screeched out of the parking lot toward downtown Jacksonville, narrowly missing a bewildered Mrs. Pickett and her poodle. While I had no idea where we were going, I raced through the quiet Saturday morning business district until we were far enough away to slow down to a reasonable speed. Still unsure where we were, I unexpectedly happened upon a diner just opening for breakfast. I parked Celia behind the building.

Lacing my fingers behind my head, I inhaled deeply and slowly exhaled.

"Good drivin', mate," said Cookie.

"Forget that. What were you doing in the other part of the building for so long?"

Cookie reached into his shirt and withdrew several folded papers. He waggled them at me.

"Are those what I think they are?" I asked, wide-eyed.

"Mate, we hit the jackpot. I've got it all right here. I was gone so long because I was trying to find paper and space to copy the documents. I found both in an office at the end of the hall."

"So, yours was the light old Mrs. Pickett saw as she walked her dog."

Cookie looked at me curiously. "Who's Mrs. Pickett?"

"Never mind. Continue."

"I had just started writing everything down when I heard voices in the foyer. I shut off the light and hid while security officers checked the offices on the first floor. When they came out of the basement and started for the second floor, I knew we could get out of the building."

"If you didn't finish copying the documents, what do you have there?" I asked, pointing to the papers. "Please don't tell me those are the originals."

Cookie gave me a sheepish grin.

I stared at my friend, unsure whether to punch or hug him. "I'm a fugitive from two counties who now possesses stolen state property. It's only a matter of time before these guys question Gina, she puts two and two together, and realizes we were the ones in the basement. She has my card! She has my name! If caught, I'll lose my reputation and license and never be able to work in law enforcement or as a P.I. again. How did I let you talk me into this?" I shook my head in dismay.

“Cheer up, mate. Let’s get some food, and I’ll show you what I found.”

CHAPTER 30

After breakfast, Cookie and I headed south for home. We stayed off State Highway 4 as much as possible in case the police had an all-points bulletin out for Celia and made our way to Palm Beach without incident. I dropped Cookie off at the restaurant and went straight home, arriving about six o'clock that night. Though exhausted physically and emotionally, I phoned Betty Lou before unpacking and told her everything that had happened and that I was home.

"Thank goodness you're safe. First thing Monday morning, we better visit Chief Borman and tell him everything. He'll understand and be able to help differ suspicion until we can sort all this out."

"Good idea," I said, my eyes beginning to close.

"I'm dying to know what the documents said. How about a hint?" coaxed Betty Lou.

"Tomorrow," I said.

"Oh, by the way, I meant to tell you something—"

"Tell me Monday," I said, not letting Betty Lou finish her sentence. "Right now, I'm hitting the hay."

~~~

Betty Lou threw her arms around my neck and tightly hugged me the second I entered the office on Monday morning. "Boss, I'm so glad you're back."

"You must have been waiting for me with bated breath," I said.

"I was. Now let's go into your office, sit down with hot cups of coffee, and you can tell me all about the documents." Betty Lou lifted my hat, hung it on the coat rack, and pointed me toward the office.

"Hey, what about this?" I asked, wriggling out of my jacket yet managing to hold on to the file folder containing Della's documents as each sleeve came off.

Betty Lou grabbed my expelled jacket and placed it over a hook. Then she ushered me forward. "I'll be right back with coffee."

As I stepped into the office, I drew my fingers over the fabric of the wingback chairs, the wooden bookshelves stuffed with books and files, and my worn desk. They seemed comfortably familiar, yet they also seemed foreign. So much had happened I could hardly believe only a week had passed. Being away seemed more like a lifetime. I sat behind my desk and set the folder on top.

"Here's your coffee." Betty Lou set my mug in front of me. "Now, let's see the documents before heading out to
~~~

see Chief Borman. I already phoned him, and he's expecting us at ten."

Betty Lou's eyes never wavered from the folder, and she licked her lips as we sat, eager to devour what was inside. I took a sip of coffee, then opened the file. But before I could share anything with her, Chief Borman and Sgt. Holcomb burst into the office, catching us unaware.

Betty Lou jumped up. "Chief! We were going to see you at ten at your office. What's all this about?" she asked.

"I'm sorry, Betty Lou, but I just received an arrest warrant from Jacksonville. Drake, please stand up and put your hands behind your back."

I knew this was coming, but I never thought it would happen in my office or Chief Borman, the man I trusted, would be the one to arrest me.

Betty Lou stood there, eyes wide and mouth agape.

I stood while the Sgt. handcuffed me. "What am I being arrested for?" I asked.

"Theft of state documents, and you're wanted for questioning by the Gadsden County Sheriff in the death of Dr. Sieler at the Florida State Hospital," said the chief.

I narrowed my eyes at the chief. "You know I had nothing to do with Dr. Sieler's death."

"That may be," said Borman, "but you need to come with us right now. And we'll take that folder." The chief reached across the desk with an open handkerchief, closed the folder, and placed it in a white paper evidence bag.

"You're making a big mistake, Joe," said Betty Lou to the chief. Then she turned to me. "Boss, don't say another word. I'll get you the best lawyer in town as quickly as possible." Betty Lou gave the chief the evil eye as he and Sgt. Holcomb marched me past her and out the door.

~~~

At the police station, Sgt. Holcomb had me empty my pockets into a small tray, took inventory of the items, and gave me a receipt. Then he took me to the processing room. I scowled at the camera and filled the fingerprint cards with inky digital imprints. Afterward, the Sgt. escorted me into a small room with a table and chairs on either side—the interrogation room—and uncuffed me.

"Have a seat," he said in his friendliest tone, which wasn't so friendly.

I sat—as if I had a choice. Holcomb sat, too. Just then, the door opened, and another officer walked in.

"Chief Borman said to give this to you." The officer handed Holcomb the evidence bag. He placed it on one side of the table.

"Now," said Holcomb, lacing his hands and resting them on the table. "I'd love to know your side of the story. I assume this has to do with the Della Carmichael case, so tell me what you were doing in the basement of the State Board of Health in Jacksonville."

"Nothing," I said, shrugging.

"Wrong answer," said Holcomb, wagging a finger at me. He pointed to the evidence bag. "That isn't nothing. Marlow, it's evidence that'll cook your goose, so you'd better answer my question."

I pretended to lock my lips and throw away the key. I knew I was being flippant, but I couldn't help myself. This guy made my skin crawl.
~~~

"Want to play hardball? I'm up for that." Holcomb opened the bag and, using a cloth, withdrew the file. He set it in front of him. "Last chance before I open the evidence and seal your fate," he said.

My gaze darted between Holcomb and the folder, and I could feel perspiration ooze from my pores. He was right. The contents of that folder would undoubtedly seal my fate in more ways than one, but I wasn't about to let him see me squirm. I set my lips in a smirk, crossed my arms defiantly, and leaned back. If this became my last stand, I would go out like Geronimo.

The Sgt. opened the file and scanned the top page. He turned the page and did the same with the next and the next. As he checked each page, bright pink moved up his neck and onto his cheeks before exploding into red blotches that covered his face.

"Is this some kind of joke?" he yelled. He stood and slapped the folder closed so hard that the pages flew out.

I jumped at his reaction, trying to comprehend what was happening. Bending to gaze at the pages, I became just as confused as the Sgt. These weren't the documents Cookie took from the basement. Several pages were blank, while others were from an outdated copy of the *Farmer's Almanac*. I couldn't help but let out a boisterous guffaw.

"This doesn't get you off the hook," Holcomb bellowed, his face so hot you could fry an egg on it. "In fact, I'll now charge you with obstruction of justice, destruction of evidence, and anything else I can think of."

"Tell me something, Sgt. Holcomb, did you see what was in the folder in my office?" I asked calmly.

He hesitated, knowing where I was going with this.

"Never mind. I'll answer for you," I said. "No, you didn't see what was in the file. You only speculated. I can't be charged with a crime if you lack evidence to support your claim." I gave him a "got you there" smile.

"We'll see," Holcomb huffed.

He snapped the cuffs back on me, grabbed my arm, and propelled me down the hall toward the jail cells. All the while, I remained baffled by what had occurred. What had happened to the original documents? How were they exchanged for blank pages and those from the *Farmer's Almanac*, a periodical staple in American homes?

Once we got to the jail, Holcomb removed the cuffs. "Have fun," he said with a sinister laugh before shoving me inside one of the cells.

I plopped onto the cot, realizing I was now on the receiving end of my time as an MP in the army and detective with the Atlanta Police Department, where I'd shoved numerous accused into jail cells. Now I knew how they felt, innocent or not.

Once the Sgt. left, I looked around. A large man stretched out on a sagging cot in the adjacent cell, his back to me. I pondered what crime he'd committed to wind up here. Probably nothing as egregious as mine. Then he turned over.

Bluto!

"It's you!" said the big man, jerking upright and staring at me with narrowed, piercing eyes. His sandpaper voice was as rough as I remembered.

"It's you!" I replied, swallowing the lump in my throat.

"You're the reason I'm here," said Bluto. His massive hands opened and closed in fists as if itching to pummel me.

"You're the reason you're here," I returned, glad bars were between us.

We stared at each other, neither willing to back down until the clang of the jailhouse door opened.

"Your lawyer's here," said Holcomb in an irritated tone. A suited man with dark hair, glasses, and sharp features followed him toward my cell.

"Mr. Townsend," said the man, sticking his long thin fingers through the bars. "I'm your lawyer."

Thank heaven for Betty Lou!

"So good to meet you," I said. "My father spoke highly of you." Townsend was the best criminal attorney in Palm Beach County now that my father had retired. I pumped his hand.

"Your arraignment is in a couple of hours. The Jacksonville police want to extradite you to their jurisdiction to stand trial. Still, I doubt your case will even go to trial, considering whatever evidence they had against you seems to have disappeared."

"Yeah, about that. We need to talk," I said in a low voice.

"I'll see you at the arraignment," said Townsend, dismissing my comment as though he hadn't heard me yet, giving me an 'I know all about it' look. He turned and exited without further discussion.

Returning to my cot, I was unsure what to do for the next few hours. Then I got a brilliant idea.

"Uh, Big Guy," I said to Bluto. "I'm not your enemy. In fact, we're on the same team."

"Humph. How's that?" he said, crossing his beefy arms over his chest. When he did, my eyes caught the sparkle of a gold ring on his right middle finger. It was in the shape of some animal, but I couldn't make out what kind.

"You thought I would hurt Della, but that was the farthest thing from my mind. She asked me to find something for her."

"And did you?" His hands now clasped his knees as he bent forward.

"Yes, that's what landed me here. By the way, I don't even know your name."

"It's Ernest, but everyone calls me, Tiny."

I swallowed my laugh. "Okay, Tiny. Since we both only want what's best for Della, perhaps we can work together to help her. If it proves successful, I may drop my complaint against you."

"I'm listening." He scooted his large carcass down to the end of his cot until we were nose to nose with only the metal bars between us. That's when I got a good look at the ring—a ruby-eyed gold alligator with a curled, horny tail that took up the length of the phalange to his middle knuckle.

"That's quite the ring," I said, pointing to the intricately designed gold reptile. "How'd you get in here with that? The cops took all my valuables."

Tiny squinted and leaned in. “Oh, I have my ways. You ever seen a gator? I mean, a really big one?” he asked.

“I’ve seen my share,” I answered. You couldn’t live in Florida and never have seen a gator.

“Then you know gators are all over Florida and eat almost anything. You ever seen one at night?”

“Can’t say that I have.”

“Their eyes glow red when you shine a light on them.” He angled his hand so I could see the light reflect off the rubies.

I wasn’t sure I wanted to hear how he knew that. I changed the subject.

Speaking in a low voice, I said, “Look, I just got back from northern Florida, where I met with several doctors from Chattahoochee. I know what happened there.” I hoped this revelation would create a chink in his facade.

“So, you know about Della and me?” His gravelly voice softened.

I gulped, trying not to show my genuine ignorance. “I know what I was told, but I’d like to hear your side of the story.” When an investigator feigned knowledge and sprinkled it with empathy, people talked.

“When she entered the hospital, it was the middle of the night. I was the orderly on duty in the women’s ward, and my boss ordered me to put her in a private room. While she got settled, we started talking. She told me about being born in the hospital, her mother dying, and how she spent time in a home in the panhandle where she grew up. Then, when she graduated, she tried to find out about her family, but some big shot in the state government didn’t want her background revealed, so he had her kidnapped and sent to the hospital."

"Did she say who this person was?"

Tiny shook his head. "She didn't know, but she swore she was going to break out of the hospital the first chance she got, find him, and expose him once and for all for what he did to her mother."

"So, one day, she did break out and made it to West Palm Beach?"

"Not exactly. Della used her physical assets to get the hospital staff to do favors for her in exchange for favors for them, if you know what I mean. It took years, but by that time, she had a plan and money."

"So she just walked out the front door?"

"No, she had help." Tiny gave me a smile of collusion.

"You helped her," I said matter-of-factly.

"Me and someone very special to her, Dr. Wilson."

"Dr. Wilson! The history professor?"

"He stayed behind at the hospital to run interference, but Della and me went to Orlando. She got a job in a dance hall there. I went on to Tampa and worked for Charlie Wall."

"The gangster?" A lump formed in my throat. Charlie Wall, who operated gambling, prostitution, and illegal numbers rackets, was Tampa's resident gangster and as dominant a figure in that central Florida city as Capone had been in Chicago.

Tiny nodded.

"Uh, do you still work for him?" I needed to know where I stood.

"Naw. I'm a freelancer now."

I didn't want to know what that meant, but I still had questions I wanted the big man to answer.

"Did you know Della's first husband with the last name of Warren?"

"Knew of him."

"What happened to him?"

Tiny gave me a toothy grin. "He died."

"Yeah, I know. But how? Why?"

"He wasn't treating Della right. Making her do things she didn't want to do."

"And." I waved my hands in the air for him to continue.

"He died. And funny thing, they never found his body."

I looked at Tiny's ring. Was Warren one of his freelance jobs? Given what he may have had to do for Charlie Wall, I wondered if Warren had met his fate in the murky waters of a local lake in the jaws of one of Florida's native reptiles.

"What about Stanley Carmichael, Della's second husband?"

"He died, too. Drowned in his pool after getting drunk." Tiny gave me a second toothy grin.

Another freelance job?

"So, what's your relationship with Della? Why did you help her?" I wondered if he was the recipient of one of her 'favors.'

"That's a private matter." He stared at me with piercing eyes that said, 'Don't ask me again.'

"Okay then."

"Does that mean you'll drop the charges?" He gazed at me expectantly.

"I'll talk to the chief about that, but he may have questions for you about other things."

"I'll handle the Chief," Tiny said, loudly cracking his knuckles and freelance written in his grin.

"No, Tiny! Chief Borman is one of the good guys. He likes Della. He'll help her." I didn't know if that was true, but despite his arresting me, I knew he'd do the right thing.

"I'll keep that in mind," said Tiny.

The door to the jail creaked open, and Sgt. Holcomb appeared. "Time for your arraignment."

He unlocked my cell, handcuffed me, and escorted me down the hall, where they had a small courtroom. The judge and Mr. Townsend were already seated. Betty Lou waved at me from the gallery. Holcomb removed my cuffs and stood close by while the proceedings took place.

~~

"What just happened in there?" asked Betty Lou as she drove me out of the police station parking lot.

"Your guess is as good as mine," I said, as bewildered as she was about Jacksonville police dropping the charges. "I'm sure it has everything to do with the lack of solid evidence. We need to talk to Chief Borman tomorrow. I'm sure he can explain."

"About Bluto," said Betty Lou. "I tried to tell you they finally got him, but you were too tired the first night, and the chief arrested you before I could say anything."

"Yeah, I know. I already spoke to the big guy."

"You what?" Betty Lou slammed on the brakes in the middle of the street, thrusting me forward and forcing me to catch myself before I hit the dashboard.

"He was in the next cell. It turns out his name is Ernest, but he goes by the name 'Tiny.'"

"Tiny? Now that's a good one." Betty Lou let out a hearty laugh.

"He's actually not that bad a guy. A bit misguided, maybe, but I think we can work with him," I said.

"Work with him? He almost killed you!"

I could practically see a geyser of steam rise from Betty Lou's ears as she continued on to the office.

"I realize this is an abrupt turnaround, but he told me how Della escaped the hospital. He was an orderly there when she came in and took pity on her. He and Dr. Wilson helped her escape."

"Her story gets more complicated by the minute," said Betty Lou, pulling into her parking space at the office.

"You have no idea," I said, holding back Tiny's employment by Charlie Wall and his alligator ring.

"Now what?" Betty Lou asked, turning to me.

"Now, you go home and relax. I'll do the same. I'll see you in the morning, and we'll pay Borman a visit." I kissed Betty Lou on the cheek before I exited the car.

Sitting behind my desk with feet up, a cigarette in one hand and my glass of whiskey in the other, I reran the day's events in my mind, still confused about the documents. When and how had they been exchanged? And who did it?

Chain of custody was one of the most critical parts of convicting someone of a crime. Evidence must be properly collected, protected, and documented. Borman took the folder from my desk and placed the file in the evidence bag. When the officer entered the interrogation room and handed the bag to Holcomb, he said it came from the chief. That meant Borman hadn't logged the evidence in, and he and the officer were the only ones to possess the bag between my office and when Sgt. Holcomb accepted it in the interrogation room. It was highly unlikely the officer would compromise the evidence; he had no connection to the case and, therefore, no motive. But if he didn't switch the papers, who did? That left the chief. But if the chief arrested me, why would he exchange the documents for worthless paper? What was his motive? And if he did, where were the records now?

I went home and fell into bed with more questions than answers. I hoped to get them when Betty Lou and I met with the chief tomorrow.

CHAPTER 31

I was behind my desk gathering my thoughts on yesterday's turn of events and staring out into the reception area when the office front door opened.

Betty Lou jumped up from behind her desk. "Chief! To what do we own this unexpected visit?"

Chief Borman, wearing civilian clothes, nodded. "I'll just pay your boss a visit," he said, turning for my office.

"Coffee?" asked Betty Lou.

"If you don't mind bringing it in there." He pointed to my office.

"Not at all," she said.

Borman strolled into my office and took a seat.

"We were planning to visit you this morning," I said, stubbing out my cigarette. "Thought we needed a chat."

“Yeah, that’s why I’m here. I didn’t want you to come to the station. It’s less official this way.”

Betty Lou brought the chief’s coffee and set it on the desk.

“You will join us, won’t you, Betty Lou?” He gave her a friendly smile.

“Of course,” she said, sitting next to him.

“I wanted to explain about yesterday’s court proceedings. I’m sure you were both confused.”

“That’s an understatement,” I said, sipping my coffee.

“Well, just before your arraignment, I got a call from the Jacksonville Police Chief. He said they were dropping all charges against you. Naturally, the only thing I could do was honor his wishes. It’s really as simple as that.”

“Did he say why?” asked Betty Lou.

“He said he got a call from the governor, and the state wouldn’t be pressing charges.” As he sipped his coffee, Borman eyed me over the rim of his coffee mug.

“My, my, wasn’t that convenient. Who do you suppose put the governor up to that?” I asked.

Borman shrugged. “He didn’t say. When the governor calls, people do his bidding, no questions asked.”

“Still, wouldn’t you like to know, Joe?” Betty Lou touched his arm and gave it a light squeeze.

“Not my business to know how or why the governor makes his decisions. Anyway, I came by to tell you you’re in the clear, Drake, and we’ve expunged your arrest record. Your friend Cookie is in the clear as well. Oh, and I spoke to the Gadsden County sheriff. He won't need to speak with you regarding Dr. Sieler's death. It's been ruled a suicide."

"Seems like there's good news all around. But what about the documents, Chief?"

"The documents? I merely had the evidence bag taken to Holcomb, so I'm not sure what you're referring to."

I knew someone switched the documents for the worthless papers, but the chief wasn't planning to tell us the whole story.

"Ah, Chief, I know this may sound strange, but I'll be dropping the assault charges against Tiny, I mean, Ernest."

"So, you two worked things out while in jail?"

"Let's just say we came to an agreement. There's no reason to keep the big guy locked up on my account, though you may wish to question him about other incidents."

"You sure about this? There's no going back once you formally sign the paperwork to drop the charge."

"I'm sure," I said.

"Okay, then. I'll have the papers drawn up. I still need to question him about Carmichael's death, and if I find any evidence he was involved, I will charge him."

"I understand, Chief."

"Give me a few days, then stop by the station and sign the papers. We still on for dinner tonight, Betty Lou?"

"Of course, Chief," she said.

The chief rose and went to the door. Just before leaving, he turned. "Have you read the morning paper?"

"Haven't gone down to get them from Willie yet," I said. "Why?"

"I think you'll find an interesting article on the front page." The chief gave us a two-finger salute and left.

"What's going on?" asked Betty Lou.

"I have no idea, but I'd better visit Willie and see what the chief's talking about. Besides, I need to pay him for finding Tiny." I grabbed my hat and left a finger kiss on the shark's tooth.

A rain storm had come through during the night, lowing the sizzling summer Florida heat to a tolerable level as I walked down the street toward Willie's paper stand. There was a spring in my step now that charges against me had been dropped, and Tiny's charges were about to be, yet there was much more to accomplish before I could close Della's case.

"Mr. Marlow. Good to see you back in town. I wondered when you were going to visit me." Willie handed me my morning papers.

I opened the *Miami Herald* to the front page. A large photo of Florida's fifty-seven-year-old governor, Adam Leighton, covered the front page along with this headline and article:

GOVERNOR LEIGHTON ABRUPTLY RESIGNS

Florida's Governor, Adam Leighton, resigned yesterday without explanation, except to say he won't be seeking a run for the White House in the upcoming national election. His announcement stunned Florida residents, staffers, and members of his party nationwide. As one of the most popular governors in the country, many believed he would emerge as the party's frontrunner for nomination for president. Now, it's anyone's guess as to who the nominee will be...

The article went on to describe Leighton's successful career in politics from city councilman to state congressman, state senator, and finally, governor. It also listed his accomplishments while governor. They were impressive.

"How does a guy who's been serving as governor for almost eight years simply resign without explanation?" asked Willie.

"Certainly is curious. By the way, thanks for your help in locating Bluto." I handed Willie an envelope with money. He stuffed it into his apron without looking inside.

"I heard you spent a few hours in jail with him."

"Word certainly travels fast around here."

"You know the Palm Beach grapevine," said Willie, wiggling his eyebrows.

"Yeah, I do. That's why I wanted to tell you that you may see the big guy around again as I'm dropping my charges against him."

"After all our hard work finding him?" Willie looked utterly baffled.

"It's complicated, but he supplied me with some much-needed information. Now it's up to the chief whether he'll keep him behind bars to ask him a few more questions. I thought you might want to alert your network, so they wouldn't think he's escaped."

"Will do," said Willie, eyeing a customer. "See you around, Boss."

Stepping into the office, I plopped the *Miami Herald* onto Betty Lou's desk, open to the front page. She stared at the headline and clucked her tongue.

"Governor Leighton resigned? I can't believe it. He's been in politics for over thirty years. Seemed to be doing a good job, and everyone loved him. Whatever possessed him to resign?"

"You never know when your past will come back to bite you," I said.

Betty Lou gazed at the governor's photo and then at my Cheshire Cat-like grin. Her eyes expanded to their fullest. "Him? Governor Leighton is Della's grandfather?" Her mouth hung open in surprise.

"When his fourteen-year-old daughter became pregnant, he didn't want anyone to know, so he sent her to the Florida State Hospital to have the baby. After Della's mother died, Leighton changed her last name and sent her to live with Ginny. When Della started getting too close to the truth after graduating, her grandfather had her returned to the hospital. He hid the truth from Della and everyone else his entire life to preserve his reputation and political career. That's why it all came crashing down once we found the document."

"But, how did he know you found his daughter's birth certificate?"

"I can't say for sure and can only surmise that Chief Borman played a pivotal role in all this."

"Joe? How?"

"I believe he's the one who exchanged the documents for the papers. I also think he called Leighton to warn him about what I'd found. If voters discovered what their governor did to his daughter and granddaughter, he could never run for president."

"So Joe tried to spare the governor the embarrassment?"

"I think it went far deeper than that. I think the chief saw an opportunity to right the wrongs done to Della and her mother and made a deal with the governor. The chief would return the documents in exchange for the governor's resignation and dropping the charges against me."

"But that doesn't make sense. You and Cookie saw the documents. You know the truth."

"Who would believe us, especially without the documents to prove it? There had to be a more permanent way."

"I know the chief, Boss. If he were involved, he could have simply asked you to keep quiet."

"Or he believed we're smart enough to read between the lines and figure out what happened without admitting he was involved and incriminating himself. As you well know, removing or destroying evidence is a crime."

"I understand," said Betty Lou. "But you're the only one who knows about the exchanged documents, which benefitted you, so there was no reason for you to talk."

"Then the only other logical explanation is the chief had compassion on Della."

"Hmm. I know you haven't spoken with her, but do you suppose she knows about Leighton?" asked Betty Lou.

"Not to my knowledge, but I'll have to tell her. That's what she paid me for."

"Not really, Boss. While I realize Della has a vendetta against her grandfather for what he did to her and her mother, when you accepted payment, you're contractual obligation was to fulfill her directive to find out who she is. Technically, it's her parents who created her, not her grandfather. She knew who her mother was but not her father. He's the one you need to find."

"You sound like an attorney," I said, stunned at Betty Lou's explanation.

"I didn't work for your father for twenty years without learning something." Betty Lou gave me a wide grin.

"Okay, then I need to find Della's father. But his name wasn't on her birth certificate, and I'm sure Leighton had everything to do with that." I ran my hands through my hair in frustration.

"Only one person knows who he is." Betty Lou pointed her index finger in the air, made two sweeping circles, and dramatically brought it down on Leighton's photo. "Another road trip?"

I sat behind my desk, contemplating Betty Lou's suggestion to visit Leighton while she returned to her desk and typed up the notes on Della's case. As I pulled open my top drawer to get a cigarette, the envelope with Della's name on the outside stared back at me. I knew what that envelope contained—Harriet's photo of her and Della as youngsters on the swing and the rope bracelet from Dr. Wilson. Both belonged to Della, and I needed to give them to her. Of course, these would only be a part of the answers she sought. The others would come when I returned from my second trip to see Leighton in northern Florida, but at least she would have these before I left. I picked up the phone and dialed her number.

"Carmichael residence," said her Chinese maid.

"Drake Marlow, here. May I please speak with Della?"

"Moment, please."

I saw that as a positive sign that Della had returned.

"Mr. Marlow," said Della, in her high nasally voice. "I take it you *finally* have news for me?"

I rolled my eyes at her jeer but restrained my tongue. "I do. Could you drop by my office tomorrow afternoon around 2:00 p.m.?"

"Sure."

"And this time, you'll show?" Given her no-show at the diner last time, I couldn't help but try to pin her down.

"I'll be there."

I hadn't seen Della in weeks and wondered where she'd been. As I thought about her and Harriet and what good friends they'd been, Constance also came to mind for some reason. Maybe because she and Della used to be friends, or, heaven forbid, perhaps I missed her smile and kind disposition.

"I'm heading to Woolworths for lunch," I said, grabbing my hat and jacket.

“I see,” said Betty Lou, peeping at me over her reading glasses.

On my way, I stopped by the florist and picked up a single yellow rose. I’d offer the symbol of friendship to Constance in hopes of continuing our intermittent relationship.

Entering Woolworths, I slipped onto a stool. Constance wasn’t behind the counter, but I was optimistic the door would swing open at any moment, and she would emerge. The door did swing open, but Irma walked through.

“Hello, Mr. Marlow. We haven’t seen you in quite a while.”

“I’ve been out of town on a case. I just got back. Is Constance here?”

“She’s in the back,” said Irma spying the rose. “Is that for her?”

I nodded.

“Oh, boy,” she said in a tone reminiscent of trouble. “Anything I can get you before I tell her you’re here?”

“The special,” I said. “With sweet iced tea.”

Irma wrote down my order on her pad, replaced the pencil behind her ear, and walked back to the kitchen. My knees nervously bounced while I waited for Constance to appear.

Suddenly, there she was—blonde hair swept back into a ponytail, aqua eyes shining, lips painted a soft pink. She took my breath away.

“Hello, Mr. Marlow.” Her voice was so melodic I could barely speak.

"Hello, Miss Grimly. I'm sorry I haven't been in touch lately. I was out of town on Della's case and just got back. Please accept this rose as my apology."

Constance smiled, brought the flower to her nose, and sniffed. That's when I caught the glint of a small diamond on her left ring finger.

"You're engaged?" My voice sounded like a scratched record.

"Mr. Wilcox."

"Of the electric company?"

She nodded, giving me an unsure smile.

"I didn't know," I said.

"How could you, though I phoned to let you know."

"That's right—the phone call just before I left. Betty Lou did say you had something important to tell me. When's the wedding?" I didn't really care to know, but I wanted to be polite.

"We haven't set a date."

Just then, Irma came from the kitchen. She set my lunch before me, gazed at the two of us, and left.

"It was nice seeing you again, Mr. Marlow. And thank you for the rose. It means a lot to me." As Constance turned and hurried toward the kitchen, her head dropped, and her shoulders shook.

~~~

"She's engaged," I said, dropping into a chair in the front office.

"Engaged, maybe, but not married," said Betty Lou, as though what I'd just told her was as mundane as putting on a pair of shoes.
~~~

I shot upright. "You knew, didn't you?"

Betty Lou shrugged. "I heard while you were away. It wasn't my place to tell you, but there's still hope as long as she's not married."

"She's engaged, for heaven's sake! Might as well be married." I leaned back against the wall and spread my arms in defeat.

"Quit feeling sorry for yourself and go after her."

"What?" I said, sitting erect.

"You like her, don't you?"

"More than I thought," I said, admitting my feelings for the first time.

"She's not married until the wedding vows and rings are exchanged. You, of all people, should know that. If you like her, go after her."

"I can't. I've been that guy, the one whose fiancé was taken away by another. And I've felt the pain. I'd never wish that on anyone."

CHAPTER 32

The next day, Della sashayed into the office at 2 p.m. on the nose, bypassing Betty Lou and swaying directly into my domain. Still wearing mourning black, her velvet hat and veil had been replaced with a broad-rimmed sun hat, and her stylish dress, flaring below the waist into a full skirt, ended mid-calf. This time, she wore black shoes. I guess she wasn't mad at Stanley anymore.

Betty Lou closed my door as I jumped up and extended my hand toward Della. "So nice to see you."

She dismissively nodded and sat, placing her clutch and gloved hands in her lap. "So, who am I?" she asked. Her ruby-red lips curled into a half grin as though doubtful I'd figured any of that out.

Knowing the image of her and Harriet would speak more powerfully than anything I could say, I pulled out the photo and handed it to her.

She blinked rapidly, holding back tears. "Sweet Harriet," she said, her gloved hand lightly caressing the photo. "Where'd you get this?"

"From Harriet."

"How on earth did you find her?" Della's eyes and demeanor softened.

"It's quite the story," I said, launching into a detailed account of Cookie's and my trip and how I found her childhood friend. "Oh, and there's one more thing. I told you about my role during the birth of Harriet's child, but I didn't tell you about the baby."

Della sat forward.

"It was a girl," I said.

"A girl!" Della squealed with delight and clapped her hands.

"They named her Della."

The room seemed devoid of air as Della sharply inhaled. Then the cascade of tears she'd held back gushed from her eyes, streaking her flushed cheeks in rivulets of mascara. I pulled a clean handkerchief from my desk and handed it to her.

"Harriet sends her love and wants you to know her door is always open. She'd love you to visit so she can introduce you to little Della."

Della's shoulders shook as the tears flowed. She dabbed her eyes with the handkerchief, her makeup smearing onto the fabric.

"The photo I gave you is only part of my trip. Here's something from a very special friend." I withdrew the rope bracelet and handed it to her.

Della took off her gloves, tenderly fingered the thin braided ropes, and hugged the precious momento to her chest. “Dr. Wilson used to braid my hair. He taught me how to braid, so I made this for him and another for me. I keep it with me always.” She reached into her purse and withdrew a second braided bracelet. “He saved me from an awful time, not just when I was a child but when I returned to the hospital after graduation. I didn’t know he was still alive.”

“He’s elderly and walks with a cane, but he’s pretty lucid. I had a wonderful conversation with him, and he doesn’t appear to be a danger to anyone. But the orderlies keep a close eye on him and don’t let him wander far.”

“Mmm,” said Della. I could see wheels turning behind her hazel eyes. “I appreciate your finding my friends, but was the trip successful? Do you know who I am?”

I knew this was coming and tried to figure out how best to broach the subject. If I told her what happened in the basement, maybe that would hold the truth off for a while. So I jumped into Cookie’s and my saga at the Bureau of Health and how we found the birth certificate. I also told her about my arrest for theft, going to jail, how the documents disappeared, and that the charges against me were dropped.

“Are you telling me you don’t know the name of my father or grandfather?”

“Your father’s name wasn’t listed on the birth certificate.”

“But my mother’s last name should have been.” Della gazed at me with stern eyes.

“I’m curious, Mrs. Carmichael, since you knew you spent your first years in the hospital, grew up with your friend Harriet, were taken back to the hospital after graduation where you escaped with the help of Dr. Wilson and Tiny, why didn't you tell me all this in the beginning? It would have given me a place to start and made the investigation far easier."

"Easier? Is that the kind of investigator you are, Mr. Marlow? Only wanting easy cases?" Her voice escalated, and I was sure Betty Lou could hear every word.

"You're twisting my words!" I felt my blood pressure rise, and heat crawled up the back of my neck.

"Am I? Tell me, Mr. Easy, who's my grandfather?"

The question sucked all the air from my lungs. "Um, I guess I'm still working on that."

"So I paid hundreds of dollars only to find out you failed." Della gathered her things as though she was leaving.

"I wouldn't say that exactly."

"I wouldn't say that at all," said Chief Borman, making a grand and unexpected entrance. Betty Lou followed the chief along with another man.

"Chief!" I said, rising. "What are you doing here?"

"I wanted Mrs. Carmichael to know her money was well spent." The chief stepped aside, revealing the unfamiliar man. "I'd like you to meet Riley Tate."

Tate politely nodded as he fingered a straw cowboy hat that complimented his attire—blue jeans, boots, and a long-sleeve shirt with a string tie. His tanned face, creased beyond its years, spoke of time out of doors, yet his smile and sparkling blue eyes softened his weathered look.

"I'm Della's papa," said Riley with a thick Florida drawl. He walked to Della, lifted one of her hands, and kissed the back of it. "You're as beautiful as Kathryn."

His admission was so abrupt Della was shocked into silence while her gaze searched his wrinkled face.

"Ah, why don't we all sit down," I said. I offered Tate a chair opposite Della and pulled in ones from the reception area for Chief Borman and Betty Lou. Once we were all settled, I said, "Chief, would you like to tell us about Mr. Tate?"

"Sure," he said. "Mr. Tate is one of the largest cattle ranchers in Florida—the Double 'T' Ranch in Okeechobee. His family has been ranching for over one hundred years and moved their entire operation from northern Florida to the Lake Okeechobee area about thirty years ago. Mr. Tate, why don't you tell them what happened before you moved."

Tate cleared his throat. His eyes took on a faraway look, and his lips curled into a broad smile. "When I was sixteen, I fell in love with Kathryn. She was the most enchanting person I'd ever met. Not only was she stunningly beautiful, but she was also gentle and kind, and when she laughed, it was melodic, like clear spring water rushing over smooth pebbles. Her father was a big shot in local government and couldn't stand to see his daughter smitten by the likes of this Florida Cracker cowboy, so he forbade Kathryn to see me. Of course, that didn't stop us. We had many secret rendezvous and swore our love to each other. We even talked of marriage, but my family moved south to Okeechobee to continue ranching there. About five months later, I returned to visit Kathryn, but her father told me he'd sent her to live with an aunt. I was heartbroken and never saw her again. It wasn't until Chief Borman contacted me several days ago that I learned that Kathryn had become pregnant, and her father sent her to Chattahoochee, where she gave birth to a baby girl. He also told me about Kathryn's death from tuberculosis. When I heard this, I broke down and cried like a baby. But then the Chief told me I had a daughter, and she lived nearby in Palm Beach. I knew I had to come here and meet her."

Tate knelt before Della, took her hands, and gazed straight into her eyes. "If I'd only known about Kathryn's pregnancy, I'd have moved heaven and earth to be with her and you. Please forgive me for not being there during your childhood when you needed me the most. I can only say I'm here now and want to make up for the lost time. Please let me get to know you, and come to Okechobbee and meet the rest of your family. They're anxious to get acquainted with you." He kissed the back of each of her hands.

We gazed at Della and held our breaths, waiting for her response.

Slowly, she withdrew her hands from Tate's grasp, then threw her arms around his neck. "Papa!" she cried, her shoulders shaking uncontrollably.

Sobs racked Della and Tate as the chief, Betty Lou, and I stood and backed quietly out of the room.

CHAPTER 33

"So, Chief, how'd you know who Della's father was or where he lived?" Extending my hand across my desk, I handed the chief a small glass of whiskey.

"I'd like to think I've developed some ability to find people after being chief for so long." He smiled and raised his glass. "To Della," he said.

"To Della," I repeated, clinking my glass against his. We both downed the Haig & Mactavish I'd kept since Cookie left it for me in the bushes after encountering the smugglers.

"So what happens with Della now?"

"She's gone with Tate to Okeechoobee to see the ranch and meet her extended family. Then I believe they're heading up to visit Harriet for a few days, and they'll stop by and see Dr. Orbach before driving to the hospital to visit

Dr. Wilson. If everything goes well, Della plans to bring him back to Palm Beach to live his final days with her."

"And Tiny?"

"He confessed to pinning Stanley Carmichael down with the skimming net but swore the man was alive when he left. I have no evidence to dispute his claim, so he's in the clear, and Stanley Carmichael's cause of death remains accidental."

"I wonder what Tiny will do now. I'd hate to think he'll go back to freelancing." The thought of bodies being thrown into the Everglades and chomped on by alligators made my stomach queasy.

"I believe he's going to stay on with Della to help out with Dr. Wilson," said the chief.

"Do you think Della will ever know about Leighton?"

"I suppose Tate will tell her the whole story when the timing's right."

When that occurred, I sincerely hoped Della could forgive her grandfather and move on with her life. With the help of Tate, Harriet, and little Della, I felt confident that would happen.

"So, Chief, what are your plans now that all the excitement is over?"

"I plan to see if a special woman who works for you is available for dinner. What about you?" said the chief, rising.

"Me? I'm heading to the Green Turtle. Cookie and I are planning our next road trip."

NOTE TO THE READER

Thank you for reading *Della*. I hope you enjoyed it. As reviews are important to every author, please take time to leave a review by going to Amazon.com and keying in Della J.J. Starling.

To become a **Preferred Reader** and receive updates and information on new releases, sign up at sallyjling.com.

ABOUT THE AUTHOR

J.J. Starling (Sally J. Ling), is an author, speaker, and historian who lives in South Florida. She writes mysteries with a Florida connection and historical nonfiction, specializing in obscure, unusual, or little-known stories of Florida history.

As a special correspondent, she wrote for the *Sun-Sentinel* newspaper for four years and was a contributing journalist for several South Florida magazines.

Based upon her knowledge as well as excerpts from her books, she has appeared in three feature-length TV documentaries—"Gangsters," the National Geographic Channel; "The Secret Weapon that Won World War II," and "Prohibition and the South Florida Connection," WLRN, Miami. She served as associate producer on the latter production. She has also appeared in and served as a production consultant for several short documentaries on South Florida history produced by WLRN, Miami.

She has been a repeat guest on South Florida PBS TV and radio stations, guest presenter at Florida Atlantic University, and guest speaker at numerous historical societies, libraries, organizations, and schools.

For information on current projects, or to become a "Preferred Reader" and receive notices on upcoming books. please visit her website at:
sallyjling.com

To engage Sally as a speaker, or to send her an email, contact her at:
info@sallyjling.com

Sally's books include:

Fiction

- *Della: A Drake T. Marlow Mystery*
- *HalfGone: A Brooks and Romero Mystery (Book 1)*
- *Frayed Ends: A Randi Brooks Mystery (Book 1)*
- *Uncovered: A Randi Brooks Mystery (Book 2)*
- *Orchid Fever: A Randi Brooks Mystery (Book 3)*
- *Capone's Keys: A Randi Brooks Mystery (Book 4)*
- *Women of the Ring*
- *Who Killed Leno and Louise?*
- *The Cloak: A Shea Baker Mystery (Book 1)*
- *The Spear of Destiny: A Shea Baker Mystery (Book 2)*
- *The Twelfth Stone: A Shea Baker Mystery (Book 3)*
- *The Tree and the Carpenter*
- *Spies, Root Beer and Alligators: Phillip's Great Adventures (Children's Novel)*

Nonfiction

- *Deerfield Beach: The Land and Its People*
- *Al Capone's Miami: Paradise or Purgatory?*
- *Out of Mind, Out of Sight: A Revealing History of the Florida State Hospital at Chattahoochee and Mental Health Care in Florida*

- *Sailin' on the Stranahan (commissioned coffee table book)*
- *Run the Rum In: South Florida during Prohibition*
- *Small Town, Big Secrets: Inside the Boca Raton Army Airfield during World War II (First and Second editions)*
- *A History of Boca Raton*
- *Fund Raising With Golf*

Made in the USA
Thornton, CO
08/06/23 18:51:22

d0f84f0d-7987-4860-b01c-4bc1c1bb5aa7R02